Smile Time Books are written for anyone who enjoys a feel-good story, and their short chapters make them ideal for reading to children at bedtime.

Other books by Robert Kingsley Hawes

The Girl I the Yellow Hat
The Jetty War

A Dog on the Run

The Magpie Way (book 2)
The Great River

When Pop Took Us Fishing

THE MAGPIE WAY

Finding Alice

Robert Kingsley Hawes

Published by Smile Time

ISBN 978-0-6452189-1-6 (paperback)

First edition, 2022

For book orders and enquiries, contact: r.hawes70@gmail.com

A catalogue record for this book is available from the National Library of Australia

CONTENTS

CHAPTER   PAGE

Chapter	Title	Page
1	Home School	1
2	Mealtime	7
3	Flight School	11
4	Poor Old Dad	14
5	The Noisy Miners	17
6	Morning Glory	19
7	Worms	23
8	Unthinkable Consequences	28
9	Mad Magpie	31
10	War	33
11	The Golden Rule of Mealtime	36
12	Charlie	38
13	Dopey	44
14	The Martial Arts	49
15	The Crazies	53
16	Nebby	58
17	Dare Devil Dopey	62
18	The World	68
19	Crossing the Line	71
20	Alice leaves	75
21	Returned from the Dead	78
22	The Rebel	81
23	Hard Times	84
24	Mayzie	86
25	Banishment	88
26	Farewell to Friends	90
27	A Different World	95
28	Never trust a Crow	98
29	Tinker and Tinkalina	102
30	Lofty the Lost	107
31	Garry the Grumpy Sheep	111
32	Skippy	114

CONTENTS

33 The Well-meaning Wildlife Park   118
34 The Land of Equal Opportunity   122
35 A Family Reunion   125
36 The Lookout   130
37 Bernard   136
38 Into the Wilderness   140
39 Homer   142
40 Trouble back Home   145
41 Journey's End   148
42 Eden Springs   152

1

HOME SCHOOL

It was a sunny spring afternoon in the newly developed suburb of Gum Tree. The houses of the Humans sat in neat rows, each roof catching the sun's rays at the exact same angle. Gum Tree lay nestled at the foot of a rolling range of hills. The early settlers had named the place Gum Tree as a tribute to the magnificent gums that grew there. But the gums were mostly gone now, pushed aside to make room for houses. Only a few remained, scattered along a creek that ran down from the hills.

At one point, several gums stood at a place where the creek made a sudden loop, leaving an awkward section of land that was unsuitable for houses. As the Humans could find no useful purpose for this plot, they declared it a nature reserve. This done, they stripped away the natural vegetation, replacing it with a rough lawn and ornamental shrubs. However, they left the gums and named the place Gum Tree Park.

To Max, Gum Tree Park was a special place, for Gum Tree Park was where he was born. Max is a Magpie, and this story begins on Max's first day at school.

Max could remember little of the first twenty-six days of his life, spent in a nest. He had some recollection of being jostled by his four siblings, all hungry and screaming to be fed. They would push their parents to the limit, but then came the night of the storm when the gentle swaying of the nest turned violent. Their tree struggled to stand upright in the roaring wind. Rain drove through the leaves, but their mother sat steadfast, holding them in, sheltering them from the rain, and keeping them warm. Max woke next morning to find that he now only had one brother and one sister. The two youngest siblings had disappeared, but Max was too young to wonder where they had gone. Their absence simply meant more food for him.

Max's schooling began on the day that he left the nest, and his perilous descent to the ground was the first test that every young Magpie must face. He knew nothing of Mother Nature's laws, but instinct told him that gravity was a force he could not ignore. One false move and he would fall, which was something he had to avoid.

Fortunately, he reached the ground without mishap. He looked up to the place from where he had come. Alas, there would be no going back. Everything that had once been below, now surrounded him, and the world now seemed a more dangerous place.

Max was greeted by his parents, and they ushered him to a tangle of undergrowth that would be his student dormitory. He was now a Home School student, but his school record already had a blemish. He had earned a demerit for being last of his brood to leave the nest.

All young Magpies are earth-bound for the first week that they leave the nest. They are at the mercy of predators and must rely on others to keep them safe. Their parents keep watch and warn of approaching danger, distracting intruders while the young Magpies hide.

Max joined his two siblings who had been awaiting his arrival. All three would be attending Home School, and their parents would be their teachers. Their dormitory was close to their nest tree and was where they would hide each night, keeping silent and still until told it was safe to come out.

Hiding was a skill that had to be learnt quickly, but the siblings found it a boring lesson. Being silent and still was simply doing nothing and doing nothing was not fun. All were restless and eager to begin flight training. However, there were several subjects on the home school curriculum and graduation was only granted once all were passed. The students were told that unthinkable consequences awaited those who did not graduate, and they wondered what this meant. Life was easy, and nothing had consequences, unthinkable or otherwise. None the less, they did as they were told, for a pass in the subject of hiding was required before they could move on.

Hiding was a lesson that did not impress Brian, who was Max's slightly older brother.

'I don't see the point of it, Squirt,' said Brian, glancing over his shoulder to make sure no adult was in earshot.

Max would have preferred not to be called Squirt, but Brian considered the eldest had the right to call the rest whatever he wanted.

'What's the big deal, Squirt? I don't see the Olds ever sitting still and being quiet.'

Their parents had just flown off, leaving the class to practice being still and quiet in their student lodgings.

'I don't understand either,' said Max, 'but I paid attention because Dad seems a little on edge.'

Shortly thereafter, their dad reappeared, swooping majestically onto the ground. He beckoned the class out of hiding. Brian was first to respond. He rushed out, mouth wide open, and his dad popped an unfortunate beetle into his greedy beak. Their dad's name was Albert.

'Where's ours?' squawked Alice and Max in unison. Alice was Max's sister.

'You were too slow,' snapped Albert. 'Your mum will be here shortly. If you are quick, one of you might get something.'

Alice looked at Max and whispered, 'Why is Brian so special? Too bad Dad did not hear him complaining about the hiding lesson. He would not be Dad's favourite then.'

Alice's whisper was unlike a Human whisper, for it was conveyed in thought, an ability Humans lost long ago. The creatures of the Natural World still have this ability. They think in a universal language, and they hear the thoughts they direct at each other. They can read a person's mind by looking into their eyes. Humans wonder how a flock of birds, or school of fish, can move as one, as if controlled by a single thought. Alas, the poor Humans are the only ones not to know the secret.

'Were you all paying attention then?' Albert snapped. 'Did you see what I just did?' Albert was the grand master of the Kingdom of

Albert, and Gum Tree Park was at the centre of his realm. He ruled over a flock of about ten Magpies.

Minor panic gripped the class. The teacher had asked a trick question, and he would demand an answer. Brian stepped to the back and hid behind Alice. Alice thought that back of the class was the place where girls stood. Losing her spot to Brian had ulterior motive stamped all over it. Max was left at the front to face the teacher.

'Well, did you?' The teacher was impatient.

'Sort of,' said Max. 'Why, what happened?'

Max stood frozen. *Not a good answer,* he thought. His mind raced in panic, bewildered by the unfairness of his situation. *How come I have to answer? Where did Brian go? Am I in trouble? Is this where I find out what unthinkable consequences are?*

Max waited for the unthinkable consequences. Instead, the teacher stood tall, pushed out his chest, and held his head high. 'Magpies are the kings of the bush, and as kings, we arrive with a majestic swoop,' he said.

Strangely, Albert's focus was on Brian, not Alice or Max, as if his words were for Brian alone. Max hoped that Brian was being singled out because the teacher thought him slow witted, but he knew that theory was too good to be true.

A question popped into Alice's mind. *Could I be a king one day?* However, Alice thought it best that she hold back her question. The teacher intimidated her, and she did not want to draw undue attention to herself.

Albert instructed the class to stay in their dormitory while he flew off to find another beetle.

Once Albert had gone, Alice turned to Max. 'What did he mean? Are we all going to be kings of the bush one day?'

Brian pushed his beak in before Max could answer. 'Don't be stupid,' he said. 'You're a girl. Dad was talking to me.'

'Are you going to be a king of the bush one day?' Alice asked.

'What do you think?' scoffed Brian. 'Have you not heard Dad tell Mum that I am leadership material and will one day lead a flock of my own? Of course, I will be a king, and if you are lucky, I might let you be one of my subjects.' Humility was not Brian's best quality.

Alice considered giving a clever response, but the moment was lost when their mum swooped in. Her name was Muriel, and this was the third year that she and Albert had raised a family in the park. Her swoop was also majestic. *Girls can do it too*, thought Alice as she pushed past her gloating brother before he could turn around. She opened her beak and accepted the offering of a small grub. *That will show him*, she thought.

Alice's little grub was bewildered. One moment, he had been crawling on a leaf, and the next moment, whack. Life changing events come swiftly in the Natural World, and the little grub was still wondering what was happening as Alice gulped him down.

Albert then returned, and this time Max got a small grasshopper. With everyone fed, snack time was over, and it was time for their first flying lesson. Max felt both excited and worried. He was the youngest and was not as strong as the others. Being last to leave the nest, he felt that he had some catching up to do.

The teacher called Brian up first and ushered him to a seat in the park. Humans sometimes sat on the seat. Sitting on things and doing nothing was something Humans did well. However, Albert had found a practical purpose for the Human's object. It made an excellent launching perch for Flight School.

'Hop onto the Human's perch,' squawked Albert.

Brian hesitated. Albert squawked his order again, and Brian jumped to attention. With a flurry of feathers, he somehow managed to lob on the seat. He turned towards his dad, looking for praise. 'Pretty good hopping effort don't you think?' he said.

Albert ignored his son's self-assessed achievement and squawked a second order.

'Fly to the ground. Spread your wings and fly to the ground.'

Fly to the ground. Spread my wings. Brian discovered the meaning of panic. He was being given too many things to think about at once. He might hurt himself. The old boy was expecting too much. Getting onto the seat had been an achievement. Brian wondered about that. *Did I use my wings to get up here?* He could not remember. He perched on the seat, contemplating the situation. Albert flew to a nearby pole from where he could watch.

Albert regarded that particular pole as his throne, the place his father had always perched when he was the grand master of the kingdom. It gave him an excellent view over the realm.

Brian continued contemplating, hoping that the old boy would eventually fly away, leaving him to simply hop back to the ground, but Albert did not move.

Finally, Brian mustered courage for the short flight. The danger was minimal, but courage was something Brian found difficult to muster. Courage took all his effort with nothing left for other things, such as planning. He leapt, giving no thought as to how wings should be spread and flapped. He face-planted the dirt, wings folded.

Alice and Max stood nearby, and they witnessed Brian's magnificent dive. They knew they would be next, but in that moment, they could only laugh. Anything bad happening to Brian was always good for a giggle.

Albert watched on from his pole. He too, had a secret chuckle. *That's the one thing I love about Flight School,* he smirked. *That first face-plant, priceless, and lots more to come.* 'Poor effort,' he squawked. 'Next time, try using your wings.'

That afternoon, the class took it in turns to jump off the seat. No one achieved a face-plant to match Brian's first, but several came close. Albert looked on, musing to himself each time an unfortunate landing occurred. The students flapped their wings, strengthening their muscles. They discovered how their wings could push the air, but they did not fly, nor come close to flying. The fact was, they did not yet have tail feathers. Soaring like an Eagle was an impossibility for their growing bodies, but they were learning to fly.

2

MEALTIME

It was a nervous night, the first night that Max slept in his student dormitory. The smells were different closer to the ground, and he missed the rustle of leaves in the canopy. Sleeping on a branch felt very grown up, but he would have preferred the gentle sway of their cosy nest. There were also the noises. They were not new noises, for they had heard them all before, but now they wondered what they were.

'What was that?' a nervous Brian kept whispering all night.

'Go back to sleep,' Max or Alice would grumble each time he woke them.

Fortunately, sleep came easy, for the day had been exhausting. However, learning did not end at bedtime. That night, Max discovered how to ruffle his feathers to keep out the cold, and the importance of Magpie solidarity, which is the obligation to always be there for one another.

With the rising of the sun came room service to their door. Hooray, some luxuries remained. Their mother stood outside the dormitory with something tasty in her beak. It was her way of getting the kids out of bed.

'First up gets a worm.' It was a trick that had never failed her.

Brian pushed aside his siblings and rushed the prize. Worms were his favourite. He savoured his reward and greedily asked for seconds. Alice and Max were equally vocal as they squawked for their firsts.

'This way,' said their mother, and they followed her into the park. Then, without warning, she became alert, her steps purposeful. She ran a short distance and pecked at the ground. Next, she stood upright and there was food in her beak. All three siblings rushed forward, mouths open and squawking. They gave no thought to how the food got there, eating it was all that mattered.

Brian got there first, but his mother ignored him. She strode towards Max and popped a small grub into his mouth. The class were being taught the etiquette of the pecking order. Every youngster must know his table manners or risk being beaten up by an intolerant adult. Their father was very good at beating up children that did not wait their turn.

Albert sat on his pole, watching out for danger. He preferred guard duty to feeding his children, for his beak had been damaged and food gathering was hard for him. This left his wife as the family's main food gatherer, and on this morning, most of the food was in hiding.

Serving breakfast took all Muriel's willpower, for she was hungry too, and her favourites were among the things she gathered. She ate some but shared the rest. Her children had to learn what everything tasted like. It takes self-sacrifice to be a Magpie mother, but then help arrived.

'Good morning, Muriel. So, this is your fine new family I have been hearing about.'

It was Jenny, Muriel's sister. Jenny was an unmarried Magpie who roamed with the other Magpies in the kingdom. She was on the lookout for a husband, but most of the males she knew were not interested. They all had excuses for not settling down. The list was extensive.

There was not enough food for everyone to eat.

There was not enough room for kids to roam.

Kids were hard work.

Albert had claimed the only suitable nesting tree.

Jenny had heard all their excuses. All the girls in the territory had heard their excuses. The girls were prepared to build the nests, but the boys could not be moved.

Muriel felt frazzled and skipped the niceties as she greeted her sister. 'Hi Jen, I could do with a hand right now.'

'Glad to oblige, Old Chook, and oh, by the way, I am pleased to see you too.'

Muriel ignored the minor chide.

Jenny looked about to see where she might find something tasty and spied a soft patch of earth in a drain that led down to the creek. She wondered why Muriel had not taken the kids there first.

'Come on kids, follow Aunty Jenny. Let's see what we can find over here.'

'Don't go there,' squawked Muriel.

'Why not?' Jenny was puzzled by the warning.

'We need Albert's permission to eat there. That's his special spot.' She looked towards her husband who was glaring down at Jenny.

Jenny swung her head in Albert's direction. 'Too bad. We all have to make sacrifices for our kids, and he can sacrifice his special spot.'

Albert seethed but remained seated on his pole. He had a broken beak, and that soft patch of earth was the only place where he could catch a worm, and he loved eating worms. But now, Jenny was feeding his private stock to his children, and with each worm fed, Albert muttered, 'That worm was one of mine.'

Breakfast was over in half the time thanks to Jenny's help. The pecking order got a bit muddled, but the siblings were all fed. Jenny announced that it was time for her to leave.

'Thanks Jenny. I don't know what I would have done without you,' squawked a grateful Muriel.

'No problem, Old Chook. It was fun feeding them, knowing that you get them back. Give me a call any time; I'm always about the place. Next time I might bring Grandma.'

Jenny flew off to her life of unattached freedom, and Muriel felt a touch of envy as she watched her go. However, Muriel's wistful thoughts were brief, for Albert swooped onto the scene. Muriel knew that she would have a grumpy husband to contend with once Jenny was gone, for Jenny and Albert had never gotten along. Jenny disapproved of Albert's ill-tempered ways and encouraged Muriel to stand up to him more. However, Muriel understood her husband well, and she knew that defiance was not the answer. What troubled her husband could not be quelled by confrontation.

Albert landed a short distance from Muriel and proceeded to step menacingly towards her. 'I don't want to see that woman back here again,' he squawked, but Muriel ignored his menacing gesture and authoritarian tone. She remained calm.

'I needed Jenny's help this morning because you were not offering,' she said.

'I was on guard duty, watching out for danger.'

Sadly, both knew that Albert performed poorly as a guard, for he had adopted a no swoop policy since breaking his beak. If an intruder appeared, he simply squawked and flew away. This disappointing attitude just added to the difficulties Muriel faced as a mother.

'You don't have to be on your pole to see approaching danger,' said Muriel. 'You can do your lookout duties from the ground and catch a few worms from your special spot at the same time.'

Albert always struggled to argue against his wife's cool logic, and he realised that he would have to do as she suggested. If he refused, Jenny would continue catching worms in his special spot, and she would get the credit.

Albert calmed himself and answered. 'Right, I will. Tomorrow morning the kids will see how a man catches worms.' Dark thoughts of Jenny then ran through his head. 'That meddling troublemaker had better have left some worms for me to catch,' he muttered to himself.

3

FLIGHT SCHOOL

Albert wanted time to unwind following Jenny's invasion of his worm patch, but Muriel needed to take a break, and she left him in charge of the class. This was good news for the siblings, for he declared it a teacher free period. The students were given their first opportunity to explore the world. However, exploration was limited to the confines of the park. Whatever lay beyond was out of bounds.

A creek bounded the park on three sides, but it was little more than a trickle linking a series of still ponds. Tangled undergrowth grew on its banks, shaded by several tall gums. The area close to the creek had a comforting casualness to it, but the park was different.

Much of the ground in the park was covered with pine bark, a mystery, because there were no pine trees. There were, however, evenly spaced ornamental shrubs with unusual smelling leaves and flowers. Beneath the shrubs were weeds, but they were withered, having met untimely deaths at the hands of the Humans. The remainder of the ground was covered in grass, but this too, suffered from the Human onslaught, for the Humans were constantly cutting the grass back to ground level with a contraption they called a lawn mower.

The Magpie flock saw the making of lawn as wanton vandalism, a selfish Human fetish that deprived some poor horse of a nice place to graze. This futile Human activity did not end there, however, for the Humans would then sit on the seat they had placed next to the lawn and watch the grass as it grew back again. Human behaviour was hard to understand.

Albert warbled his students to gather around, the Magpie equivalent of ringing the school bell. The teacher free period was over. Alice was first to class. She was having a good morning. Her mum's masterful handling of her dad had been the highlight. *You can't push girls around,* she inwardly smiled. *I hope Brian was watching.*

11

Albert stood his class in line and gave each student their assessment from the previous day's flying.

Alice: She gave a good effort considering the fact that she was a girl.

Max: He needs to build up his strength but will never have what it takes to be a leader.

Brian: He has great athleticism and leadership potential. True, he had some difficulties, but he should not be discouraged. Magpies never fly on day one.

Alice and Max looked at each other, both thinking the same thing. *Magpies never fly on day one. Now he tells us.* They were annoyed that only Brian was receiving praise. It appeared that he could do no wrong.

Alice and Max did not like Brian. He had been a bully in the nest and had successfully fought to get the greatest share of food. That was how he had become the strongest. He was his father's favourite son. Charm and cuteness counted for nothing. Screaming the loudest and pushing your open beak firmly into your parent's face was what won you favour. Brian was an expert. Max had a suspicion that Brian was somehow involved in the mysterious disappearance of the two who vanished on the night of the storm, but crime and punishment are unknown concepts in the Magpie world.

Albert announced that they were to move to the next phase in flight training, and he marched his class to one of the ornamental shrubs. 'Welcome to Flight School Gymnasium,' he said in an ominous tone.

The siblings looked at each other. *What's a gymnasium?* they wondered, but Albert gave no time for questions. He squawked his next order.

'Get in there and jump between the branches, and don't let me see any of you slip. No one learns to fly until they can land on a branch.'

Albert ran Home School as though it was boot camp, and he enjoyed the role of nasty drill sergeant.

'Too easy,' said Brian. 'Give us something hard to do.' Brian was sucking-up to the teacher.

'It will get harder,' squawked Albert. 'By the end of the day, I want to see you jumping so far that you will have to use your wings. Points will be deducted for crash landings.'

'Why is there a penalty for crash landings?' Max asked. He already had a demerit on his school record, and the prospect of earning another seemed unfair.

Albert placed a wing on Brian's shoulder. His voice softened, but it still sounded ominous.

'Brian knows the importance of landing, but the rest of you were too busy giggling to learn from yesterday's lesson. Brian's excellent demonstration of a crash landing taught him the most valuable lesson a flyer will ever learn. Flying will never hurt you, but disaster always lurks when landing.'

'Only a teacher's pet gets praised for failure,' Alice whispered to Max.

Albert flew to his pole, the throne where he always felt masterful. He was happy that Muriel had left him in charge of Flight School. He relished the role of Flight School instructor because it required little effort on his part, other than to watch. Being entertained by crash landings was the bonus, and deducting points was his speciality.

The students surveyed the bush that was the gymnasium. Its branches provided nicely spaced perches for jumping, and Brian felt eager for the challenge. He was the strongest, could jump the furthest, and could grab a branch the firmest. He was about to shine in the teacher's eyes. More praise awaited.

Albert sat majestically on his throne and looked down at his young students. At first, they hesitated, summing up each landing target and the distance to be jumped. As the morning went on, they got better. They challenged themselves, hopping from lower to higher branch, and then from higher to lower branch, and then between branches that were further apart. There were a number of crashes and tumbles, and Albert enjoyed each little mishap as he deducted a point.

4

POOR OLD DAD

Unfortunately, all good things must come to an end, and Albert's enjoyment ended when Muriel returned with Jenny.

'We're here to feed your kids,' Jenny taunted, as Albert joined them on the ground. He scowled and walked away, trying not to show his annoyance.

'Shush, Jenny,' said Muriel. 'Albert has volunteered to provide all the worms for tomorrow morning's breakfast.'

'That's a show I don't want to miss,' Jenny laughed. 'There won't be too many worms on the menu I am guessing.'

Jenny felt that she could risk annoying Albert, for she was Muriel's sister and was helping to feed his children. But she was wrong, for mocking Albert in front of his children was crossing the line. He let out a loud squawk and rushed at her. Jenny got the hint and spread her wings. 'Goodbye everyone,' she cried. 'I'll be back when someone is in a better mood.'

Muriel frowned at Albert. 'Look what you have done now,' she scolded. 'I have lost my only helper.'

Albert looked away, for he was not prepared to have another argument with his wife. He flew to his man tree, the place that was his sanctuary.

There had been a time when Albert had commanded great respect, but his broken beak had changed all that. He now had trouble feeding himself and had to rely on others to feed his children. But no one made allowance for his disability or knew the torment he suffered from the endless flashbacks that replayed the moment of his injury.

'What happened to Dad's beak?' Alice asked, once he had left.

Muriel shook her head. 'Don't ask. Never ask. He made up a stupid story no one believes, and he won't tell us what really happened.'

The siblings looked at each other. They were curious about their dad's disfigurement, but an upset dad was something to be avoided. Perhaps they would never know. The disfigurement made him look angry. It had to be a battle scar, and they wondered who his adversary had been.

Albert had left Muriel to feed the children on her own. She gathered the class and told them to be still and quiet.

Why are we being still and quiet? thought Brian. *There is no point in doing the hiding lesson when we are standing in the open.* 'Hey, Squirt, tell Mum people can see us,' Brian whispered to Max.

'Don't do it, Maxie. He only wants to get you into trouble,' Alice cautioned.

Without warning, Muriel rushed past Brian and rammed her beak deep into the ground.

Oh no, thought Brian. *Mum has gone nuts. No one does that. I am certainly never going to do that.*

Muriel began to wriggle her head, and next, she popped back up with a plump, white grub in her beak.

Wow, thought Max, *a magic trick. How did she do that? I bet she had the grub in her beak the whole time.*

'Can I have it please,' asked Alice, who knew that her mum was always fair.

'No, it's mine,' squawked Brian. 'I am the best student in the class. I deserve it the most.'

Muriel swallowed the grub, and Max saw no magic this time. He already knew how to make a grub disappear. *What a greedy mum*, he thought, and then he squawked, 'Make another appear. That was such a good trick. We all want a grub.'

'It was not a trick,' scolded Muriel. 'Were you not all watching?'

'I was worried that you had hurt yourself,' said Alice, 'and Brian was trying not to giggle.'

'Was not,' scoffed Brian. 'I thought Mum had tripped.'

Brian gave a disapproving glance towards his sister and then began pecking at a twig lying on the ground. That twig was suddenly the most important thing in Brian's life, for Brian had a short attention span.

'Pay attention, Brian. You all need to learn this lesson, or you will starve.'

Their mum's harsh tone was as severe as their dad's.

How could we starve? thought the siblings. *People bring us all the food we can eat.*

Muriel broke into another trot, stopped, and then rammed her beak into the ground for a second time. After several head wriggles, she stood back up, empty beaked. Max was disappointed. His mum had forgotten how to do the magic trick.

'Grubs are sometimes difficult to dig out of the ground as the day gets warmer,' Muriel explained. 'I think we will have to settle for small beetles in the grass.'

'What about worms?' asked Alice. 'Aunty Jenny gave us lots of worms this morning.'

Muriel shook her head. 'No, from now on, you will have to ask your father if you want a worm. Worms will be his speciality.'

Everything seemed a mystery to the siblings. They had no idea how their parents made food magically appear, or why the Humans meddled so strangely with Mother Nature's things. Nor could they understand why their dad disliked Aunty Jenny, or why she had to leave in such a hurry. There was so much more to be learnt at Home School than just flying, and they wondered if they would ever understand it all. But fortunately, their mum appeared to know all the answers and she would have to be the one that they looked to for guidance.

5

THE NOISY MINERS

Gaining and holding territory is an endless struggle in the Natural World, for every creature needs a place to call home, and Gum Tree Park was home to many. It was their final refuge, for all else had been destroyed by the encroachment of the houses. The Humans had chopped down most of the trees with no regard to those who made the trees their home. But the Human invasion had also brought new birds to the district. Sparrows appeared not long after the Humans arrived, and the Sparrows were quick to settle in. These happy little birds got on well with everyone, but sometime later, a less friendly type of bird arrived. These were the Noisy Miners, and they wanted the place for themselves.

The Noisy Miners once lived in far-off communes, but something had changed in the environment, causing these nasty warriors to march and multiply. Some blamed the Humans, whose habit of felling trees had cleared the way for the Miners to advance.

Unfortunately, the Miners had no desire to share the territories they gained and forced out whatever birds they could. The Sparrows were among the first to leave, along with most other small birds. However, some more robust birds did find ways to stay. The peace-loving Doves used their negotiating skills to draw up an agreement for Doves and Miners to live together. Others, such as the Murray Magpies and Black Birds, kept out of the Miners' way. At Gum Tree Park, only the Magpies stood their ground. They would not be moved.

Each evening, a warning cry would envelop the treetops, the shrill chorus of the Miners telling other birds to roost elsewhere, the trees belonged to them. But the Magpies simply ignored these warnings, which was an affront to the Miner's reputation as fighting men.

The Miners next line of attack was to swoop their adversaries, but the Magpies knew how to duck for they were expert swoopers themselves. The Miners soon found that swooping a swooper was futile, for swoopers always swooped back. Swooping exchanges were common but were more a sporting contest than a battle.

The Miners sometimes tried mobbing tactics, where a group would surround a solitary Magpie while he was eating something on the ground. One would taunt the Magpie, and if the Magpie gave chase, the rest would move in and grab the food. However, the Magpies were aware of the trick and seldom moved far from what they were eating. These standoffs usually ended when a second Magpie arrived on the scene.

The second Magpie would pay no attention to the food, for he had to comply with the pecking order. His focus would be on the Miners, and if he caught one, that Miner would discover the damage that a sharp Magpie beak can do.

Sometimes, the Noisy Miners used a tactic of subtle harassment. A lone Miner would follow a Magpie wherever he went, but the harassed Magpie usually ignored the unwelcome company and simply went about his business.

In many ways, jousts between Miners and Magpies were more about pride than territory, for the Miners saw some value in having the Magpies for protection. From time to time, a Falcon would foray into Gum Tree Park, hunting for a kill. The Miners would take to the treetops and hide, shrieking their shrill warning. None would come out to fight, but the Magpies would rally together and drive the intruder away.

6

MORNING GLORY

The Welcome of the Dawn is a ceremony as old as the Natural World itself, and Magpies celebrate this ritual every morning. The siblings had been hearing it since the day they were born. Max would have preferred more sleep, but the responsibilities of his parents always prevented this. It was as if their dad stayed awake all night, waiting for the dawn to appear. He would look towards the place from where the sun rises, and when the sky began to glow, the dawn song would begin.

The world of the Magpie was ruled by the sun; they lived in its light and were nurtured by its warmth. When it slept, they slept. The Magpies understood the sun's moods. They knew the world was warmest when the sun was highest in the sky and was coolest when it slept beneath the ground.

The sun controlled life's cycle. There was the Living Time when the sun grew in strength. This was the time when birds, animals, and insects, were born. Trees sprouted new leaves, flowers bloomed, and fruit appeared. Then the sun would need time to rest. This was the Dying Time.

The Dying Time was a cold and dreary time. The trees lost their leaves, the fruit disappeared, and succulent delicacies, like caterpillars, were no more. The creatures of the Natural World often struggled to find food in the Dying Time, as everyone waited for the next Living Time to begin.

For the siblings, the Dying Time meant nothing. To them, the world was an exciting place, full of life. There was so much to explore, and so much fun to be had. They were keen to learn to fly, but their other lessons seemed of little importance. Fortunately, their parents knew the importance of all their lessons. They knew what was needed to survive the Dying Time that was coming.

***

19

The siblings stirred in their student dormitory, for another day was about to begin. The shroud of darkness was lifting, and familiar objects were once more taking shape in the park. Towards the hills was the glow that would herald the sun. All was silent and still, but not for much longer. It was time for their dad to take centre stage and commence the ceremony.

Albert believed that it was a Magpie's destiny to sing to the rising sun because no other creature had the talent. 'It's the Magpie's duty to welcome the sun,' he would say. 'If we do not welcome him, he might not bother to return.'

The welcoming time had come once more, and the glorious notes of the majestic Magpie resounded across the houses. The siblings shook their feathers, blinked their eyes, and looked at each other. Brian was not a morning person, and he was cynical about anything his dad thought important.

'Why do we need to put up with all this? Listen to the old boy, carrying on like a pork chop. Doesn't he know that people are still trying to sleep?'

'What's a pork chop?' Alice asked, giving her cynical brother a querying look.

'I don't know,' said Brian. 'All I know is that I have heard Mum say that Dad carries on like a pork chop, and I think I know what she means.'

Max was perched to one side, listening to his dad's rendition. Brian's words prompted him to join the conversation.

'Well, I think Dad sounds great. I hope I can sing like that one day.'

'It's called carolling, Squirt, and you will never be able to sing as good as I can,' scoffed Brian.

Being the oldest, Brian claimed superiority in all things. Being the youngest, Max claimed the right to be the most annoying.

'You can't sing,' Max laughed.

'Can so.' The grumpy morning person would not be contradicted.

'Cannot.' Max was determined to annoy his brother.

'Can so.'

The argument continued.

'Cannot.'

'Can so.'

'Prove it.'

'You prove I can't.'

'You prove you can.'

'You prove I can't.'

Alice was becoming sick of her brothers' squabble. 'Boys, stop it. I am trying to listen to Dad.'

But Max was determined to have the last word. 'You prove you can.'

'SHUT UP!' squawked Alice, her words sounding much louder than intended.

Sometimes, young Magpies can find themselves in need of a child protection agency, but such agencies do not exist in their world. From that moment on, Alice's relationship with her father would never be the same. The sound of his daughter's voice and those cutting words, 'shut up', caused Albert to miss a note in his glorious rendition. Brian and Max both looked at Alice.

'You're in trouble now,' Brian laughed.

This is so unfair, thought Alice. *Brian is the troublemaker, but it is always Max or me who gets into trouble. I hate him.*

Alas, Brian was correct. The first rays of the sun had barely touched the tops of the houses before his prediction came true. Alice found herself sprawled flat on her back with her dad's claws sunk deep into her chest, his full weight on top of her. 'Never, never, never, interrupt the dawn ceremony again,' he squawked.

Albert always repeated his words whenever he was angry, and he was very angry. 'You have made me a laughing-stock. Thank goodness there were no Kookaburras around,' he shouted.

Alice lay pinned to the ground, gasping for breath.

'What's a Kookaburra?' Max asked, purposely trying to interrupt what was happening.

'Keep out of this,' Albert snapped.

Muriel stepped in and answered the question. 'A Kookaburra is a very gallant bird. In many ways, they are like Magpies. I like Kookaburras.'

As always, Muriel's words had an immediate impact on her husband. Alice was released, for Muriel now had Albert's full attention. Albert hated the fact that the Kookaburras claimed that they were the kings of the bush. 'You and your Kookaburras. They are stupid birds,' he growled.

Albert was again caught in a war of wits that he could never win, for Muriel knew all his buttons, and she knew when to press them. The Kookaburra button saved Alice from injury, for it invoked Albert's obsession that Magpies were better than Kookaburras. She continued her praise of Kookaburras. 'Kookaburras are very clever birds. Humans have even been known to imitate their call. I have heard that they sometimes kill snakes.'

Muriel's words infuriated Albert. 'That Kookaburras kill snakes thing is a myth,' he squawked. He glared at her and then flew to his man tree.

Alice was saved from possible injury, but the damage was done. She was now the official bad child of the family.

Max turned to his sister. 'I'm sorry, Sis, I should never had tried to have the last word.'

'That's okay,' said Alice. Then, with a look that only an angry sister can give, she turned to Brian. 'I hate you!' she squawked.

7

WORMS

The students enjoyed the rest of that day, mostly because their dad was not there. He spent the day brooding in his man tree, leaving his wife to look after the children. Fortunately, Aunty Jenny was soon on the scene, and this time Grandma was with her. The trio served the breakfast previously promised by Albert, and then schooling began. The siblings enjoyed the extra attention, particularly the applause they got each time they achieved a personal best. A good day was had by all, but the issue of the morning's event was not yet over. The day that followed was the day that changed everything.

That day began as always, with the students perched in their dormitory, listening to the dawn ceremony. They could still hear the anger in their dad's voice, and they hoped he would spend another day in his man tree.

The ceremony ended, and they waited for breakfast. They waited, and they waited. Brian became restless. 'Do you think that they have forgotten that they have kids? They are getting rather old you know.'

No one bothered to answer. They just kept peering through the leaves, waiting for their mum to arrive, but it was their dad who appeared, and he had nothing in his beak. Punishment was about to begin.

'Where's our breakfast?' squawked Brian.

'Room service is off for the morning,' snapped Albert. 'You all need to be punished for failing to respect your elders.'

The siblings sat silent as they wondered what this meant. Alice blamed Brian for their punishment, for he had started the argument the previous day. Brian blamed Alice for her outrageous outburst, and Max blamed himself. If only he had not been so stubborn. They clung to their perches, feeling stressed, but none knew that their dad was feeling the most stressed of all.

Albert had suffered a great humiliation, for the flock had heard Alice cause him to miss a note during the morning ceremony. Added to this, his children had seen Aunty Jenny mock his ability to catch worms. People were expecting him to fail again, and it would probably happen because he had yet to fulfil his promise to catch worms for breakfast.

His fate now lay with the worms in his worm patch, and shame would follow if his worm hunt failed. Always a thinker, however, he had devised a backup plan should this happen, but it relied on Brian, and that was what stressed him the most.

He ordered the class out of their dormitory and marched them to his worm patch. 'As punishment for yesterday's interruption of the dawn ceremony, you will have to beg for your breakfast this morning, and I will decide which of you are worthy of a worm.'

He began clawing at the ground, looking for tell-tale holes and trails, but found nothing. His worst fears were realised. Aunty Jenny had destroyed his worm patch. Any worms that had survived her onslaught were now in hiding. This meant that he would have to enlist Brian's help to carry out his contingency plan.

'Where are the worms?' asked Brian.

'You will see the worms shortly,' Albert squawked, 'but Alice and Max are to be punished. They will go over there and fossick in the pine bark. That can be their punishment.'

The disgraced pair dropped their heads. They saw no point in fossicking because no one ate pine bark. Food only came from the beaks of grownups.

Albert watched them wander to their place of punishment, and then he whispered to Brian, 'There are no worms in the park today, but we are going to pretend that there are. We will make the others think that you are eating worms, but you must keep our game a secret. This is your secrecy test. Once the game is over, I excuse you from all other schoolwork until tomorrow.'

Brian hated schoolwork, particularly the hiding lesson, but this secrecy test came with a teacher free day. The reward bought his silence. Meanwhile, Muriel was curious to see how her husband was handling things, and she landed on the pole that was his throne. From there, she could see everything, and she was bemused. Alice and Max were standing, doing nothing, while Brian was following his dad like a little puppy.

'I have a worm, Brian,' Albert shouted, and Brian opened his beak.

'Thanks Dad, that was a lovely tasting worm. Got any more?'

Muriel blinked her eyes. She saw no worm.

'I have got another worm,' Albert squawked once more. He looked across to Alice and Max. 'How are you kids going over there? Found anything nice to eat?'

'We don't know how to make worms appear,' Max complained.

Brian laughed. 'That shows how much you know, stupid. Dad says that there are no worms in the park today.'

Brian never missed a chance to belittle his siblings, but he was not the smartest of Magpies. He was saying that there were no worms in the park after pretending to eat one.

Albert glared at Brian. 'We are making them think that we are catching worms,' he whispered.

'Sorry, Dad, I forgot.'

Brian ran to the edge of the lawn fearing the consequences of his mistake, but dealing with his foolish son was not what troubled Albert. His plans were falling apart. He needed another lie to get himself out of trouble. 'I have just caught the last worm in the park,' he squawked.

There was silence as everyone wondered where the worms had gone, and then a fabulous thing happened. Max saw a movement a short distance away. A piece of pine bark had given a wriggle. He rushed over and pushed the bark to one side. Beneath it was a tail, rapidly disappearing into the ground. Max had never seen a whole worm, but he had imagined how they looked each time a grownup had popped one into his beak. However, his dad had said that there were no worms in the park. Max hesitated, wondering who owned the tail, but then curiosity got the better of him. He clamped his beak on the disappearing target and did his best to tug its owner out of the ground. Alice ran across to see what Max was doing. In the silent language of the Natural World, Max said, 'I think I have a worm.'

'Max has got a worm. Max has got a worm,' squawked Alice, repeating herself, a trait she must have inherited from her father. Albert and Brian looked in her direction.

'Quiet, Sis, I only think I have a worm. I haven't got it yet.'

But Alice could not hold back her excitement. 'Get it, Maxie, please get it, and if it is big enough, can we share?'

The suggestion that food might be on offer was enough to get Brian's attention. He ran across to watch.

'Come back, Brian,' snapped Albert. 'There are no worms over there. Stay here with me.'

The probability of Max catching a worm was something Albert had not anticipated. His contingency plan was now in total disarray.

Max kept pulling, but the creature held firm. Suddenly, snap, poor creature in the ground, for it departed from its tail, which was now in Max's beak. Max thought for a moment. *What do I do with it?* Then the flavour came through, and he needed to think no more. He swallowed. It was delicious, perhaps the most delicious thing he had ever tasted, but that was most likely because he had caught it himself. He stood, looking down at the tiny hole the creature had made. Albert ran over to put an end to all the fuss.

'No worm I see,' smirked Albert.

'It tasted like a worm,' gasped Max.

'We don't see it,' laughed Brian.

'I don't think you had a worm,' said Albert, shaking his head. 'There are no more worms in the park today.'

Max said no more. His dad had said that there were no worms, but he had just eaten a worm's tail. He looked again at the tiny hole in the ground, and then thought about the grownup's magic trick. *Now I know how the trick is done,* he thought. *They hide the food in little holes like that one.*

Albert decided that it was time for him to leave. Nothing was going right, and Muriel was beginning to annoy him. She was sitting on his throne that was his exclusive perching spot. He looked at Brian and gave a departing caution. 'Remember your secrecy test. Fail, and you will be punished.' With warning given, he left to reclaim his throne.

Muriel saw him coming and anticipated her impending eviction. She flew down to join her children. As the two Magpies passed mid-air, Albert growled, 'I don't appreciate people spying on me.'

Muriel landed alongside Max. 'You did have a worm, Max, I saw it,' she said.

'I know,' Max replied.

'I saw it too, Maxie,' Alice added, excited by her brother's success.

Brian was not sure whom to believe. They were saying it was a worm, but his dad said that there were no worms in the park that day. He was confused.

'Time for a flying lesson,' their mother announced, changing the subject.

'But we are hungry,' Alice protested.

'Your father wants you punished and so you will have to eat later,' Muriel answered.

The siblings looked at their dad who was glaring down from his throne.

'Can we have worms later?' Alice asked.

'Not today,' said her mother. 'Your dad said that there are no worms.'

'But Max found a worm,' Alice protested.

Muriel shrugged. 'Trust me, if your dad said that there are no worms, then we should not go looking for them.'

Why are men so difficult? thought Alice, but she guessed her mother was still figuring that out for herself.

8

UNTHINKABLE CONSEQUENCES

Muriel called the class to order. 'Today, we will practice taking off from the ground,' she said. 'Magpies spend a lot of time on the ground and knowing the correct method of take-off is very important.'

'But how can we take off if we cannot fly?' Alice asked. Alice liked her mother being the teacher because she could ask her questions, whereas her dad frightened her.

'Just run into the breeze,' her mother answered. 'Spread your wings and see how high you can jump. You will feel the air try to lift you. Don't worry about flying, your wings are not strong enough, but they soon will be.'

A light breeze was wafting through the park, making the lawn an excellent runway. The siblings faced the breeze, they ran, they jumped, they flopped, and they face-planted. Aunty Jenny and Grandma arrived to see how they were going. Brian was first to greet them. 'We're hungry,' he squawked. 'Can you feed us?'

Muriel was quick to explain that Albert was punishing the children. He was denying them their breakfast, having found them guilty of disrespecting his authority.

Grandma was not impressed. 'What absolute nonsense,' she squawked, and she glared at Albert who was staring down at her.

Aunty Jenny agreed with Grandma. 'I don't know why anyone puts up with that grumpy old man. Starving children is child abuse. Come on kids. Let's see if we can find a worm where we found them yesterday.'

Albert was horrified. 'That Jenny is out of control,' he muttered.

Everyone's attention was now on Jenny, and no one noticed two boys walking towards the park. They were planning to have a game of catch.

Suddenly, Muriel saw the danger.

'Run to your dormitory and be still and quiet,' she squawked.

Alice and Max did as they were told, and scrambled to their dormitory where they crouched motionless, peering out through the branches, but Brian remained where he was.

'Run and hide like you have been taught,' Muriel squawked once more.

'I don't have to do schoolwork today,' Brian declared.

Meanwhile, his dad was fixated on Jenny, fretting that she might find a worm. He did not see the boys until it was too late. 'Run, Brian, Humans are coming,' he shouted, and then he flew off to his man tree. An irrational fear of Human boys was one of the many dark monsters that stalked inside Albert's head.

Brian heard his father's warning, turned, and saw the danger. He ran, flopped, and tumbled.

'It's a Magpie with a broken wing, get him!' one of the boys shouted. They chased Brian who took refuge in the gymnasium bush.

The boys began to shake the bush.

'Stay in the bush,' squawked Muriel, who was trying to draw the boys' attention.

The taller boy glanced in her direction. 'Watch the other Magpie, it might swoop us,' he said.

Sadly, swooping was the man's job in Brian's family, and the boys were safe because the man had flown away. This left Brian to save himself, and so Brian did what Brian did best—he panicked. *I bet I can fly*, he thought.

Brian was a good athlete, but he struggled in the subject of sensible choices. He rushed out of the bush and ran as fast as he could, flapping his wings as he went. He turned to face the wind with the boys in close pursuit. Then he tripped, performing a double somersault that would have made any athlete proud, but it was not part of his take-off plan. A Human hand was soon wrapped around his body, trapping his wings. A second hand then clamped his beak.

'What shall I do with him?' Brian's captor yelled.

'My uncle works at a wildlife park. We should ask him,' his friend replied.

'Good idea. Let's go and find a box to put this Magpie in.'

Alice and Max now knew the reason for their hiding lesson, and Brian had paid the price for failing to do his schoolwork. They watched the boys leave with Brian struggling in the grip of Human hands.

'I feel terrible for telling Brian that I hated him,' said Alice, discovering the feeling of guilt for the first time. 'Do you think we will ever see him again?'

'Probably not,' said Max, 'but none of this was your fault. Brian caused it all himself.'

'I know,' said Alice, 'but I just wish that none of this had happened.'

No more was said.

9

MAD MAGPIE

Albert was in serious trouble. His family of five offspring was now down to two, and people would all blame him. He had no choice other than to take a firm grip on his perch and listen to his wife as she listed his many faults. He protested that much of the criticism was unfair. He had done his best and could not be blamed for the storm that took two of their children, and Jenny was to blame for Brian's capture. He would have seen the Humans coming had she not distracted him.

'You cannot blame Jenny,' Muriel snapped. 'You were behaving badly, and you failed in your duty to be our guard. A better man would have swooped those boys, but you just flew away.'

No one understood Albert's fear of boys. Boys annoyed him with their shouting and the way that they ran everywhere. He worried about them climbing trees and throwing stones, but he no longer talked about why he feared them, for that would involve telling once more the story of his broken beak.

Albert had claimed that a boy had been responsible for the trauma that now darkened his soul, but he had no idea what actually happened that day. He had woken under a pile of leaves, his head in pain, and his beak broken. Before that, he recalled a boy staring at him, holding an object in his hands. Albert suspected that the boy had somehow used the object to snap his beak and knock him unconscious. The boy had then buried him under leaves.

Everyone dismissed Albert's story as implausible because no one knew about slingshots, those devious devices that boys use to harass Mother Nature's creatures. Everyone assumed that Albert had broken his beak in a reckless act and was making up lies to cover his embarrassment.

Albert could do nothing about those who mocked him behind his back, but he made certain that everyone feared him to his face. He had become a bully, for people must always show respect to the grand master.

However, Albert now had a new problem to plague his troubled mind. He had denied responsibility for Brian's capture, but his conscience was telling him otherwise. Fortunately, no one knew that Brian had failed to run to safety because of the bribe he was given, but Albert would now have to carry that guilt. His troubled mind needed someone else to blame, for it was pointless blaming Jenny.

That afternoon, he wrestled with this problem as he sat in his man tree. He needed a soft target on whom to take out vengeance but could think of none other than the Humans. They were to blame. With newfound courage, he glared at their houses, spread his wings, and declared war on them all.

10

WAR

Albert returned to the park and found his children doing their schoolwork. He sat on his throne and watched them perform small leaps inside the gymnasium bush. Muriel was standing guard. Finally, the students could leap no more.

'Can we do something else, Mum, my legs are tired?' Alice pleaded.

Albert heard Alice's plea and thought to himself, *They need to work harder than that*, but he was not about to interfere. He was there to do something far more important than teach his kids to fly. He was waiting for a Human to appear.

Muriel turned to her class, 'Let's go and explore the creek.'

The idea appealed to everyone but Albert. He would have to interfere after all. 'NO!' he squawked. 'Everyone must stay in the park.'

Muriel looked up, surprised that her husband had returned. 'The kids need a break,' she yelled. 'They have earned a school excursion.'

'You will all stay where you are until I say you can leave,' Albert ordered. The firmness of his tone left little room for argument.

Muriel sighed. She saw no logic in Albert's demand, but she had done enough arguing with him for one day. She was currently ahead on the argument scoreboard, for their last argument had ended with him going to his man tree. His retreat meant that she had scored a victory, but her instinct told her that she should quit while she was ahead.

Muriel turned to her class. 'Go for a wander on the lawn and see what you can find. We will do some exploring later.'

She guessed that her husband was no longer feeling guilt for his failures, and she was right. Albert's guilt had turned to anger, an anger that he could only quell by swooping a Human, and he wanted everyone to witness the vanquishment of his first victim. From now on, he would swoop every Human that came to the park. That was how he would avenge Brian's capture. His swooping would have nothing to do with the protection of children, it was being driven by his troubled mind.

A short time later, Pastor Smith arrived for his regular park visit. The park was where he came to get inspiration for his sermons. He strolled towards the seat at the edge of the lawn, the words of his next sermon already gathering in his head. *I should talk about rebirth and springtime,* he thought. *Mother Nature has truly blessed this day.*

Albert squawked a warning, 'A Human is coming,' but this time he did not fly away.

The siblings ran and hid in their dormitory while their mother ambled in the opposite direction. But Albert stayed put, the blood rushing through his veins. He glared at the pastor whose heart was filled with the joy of spring, unaware that war had just been declared.

Albert swooped, a glorious, textbook swoop, gaining speed as he closed in with purpose. He levelled, adjusted the angle of attack, took aim at his target, and struck.

The pastor suspected nothing, for all was happening behind him. Suddenly, he felt a wing brush across his head, a blast of air around his neck, and he heard the click of a Magpie beak in his right ear. The pastor stumbled, threw his arms over his head, and ran out of the park. Albert was the victor, and he felt invigorated. He flew back to his throne and watched his victim retreat down the road.

'Darn my broken beak,' Albert mumbled. 'I wanted to make a louder click than that.'

***

When Pastor Smith delivered his sermon that following Sunday, he did not talk about rebirth and spring, he talked about forgiveness. He told how he had forgiven a Magpie who had attacked him, and he reminded his parishioners that there is good and bad in all of us.

'Bad things come from bad deeds done,' he told them, 'but forgiveness brings a new beginning. Good things will come when good deeds are done.'

However, forgiveness was not what filled Albert's heart. He was still rejoicing in his victory. Swooping a Human had been less hazardous than he thought, and he wondered why he had never done it before. Swooping could solve all his problems, for it would earn him great respect from the flock. He had found a way to wage a war that only he could win, because Humans could not fly.

11

THE GOLDEN RULE OF MEALTIME

It took a week for Alice and Max to learn how to fly. At first, they covered short distances, but as each day passed, their wings grew stronger, and they flew further. Their tail feathers grew which gave them balance in the air. With proper tails, they looked more like Magpies. They still had their school uniforms with mottled markings, but the blemishes were going. Soon, they would be magnificent, black and white birds that could wheel through the air with grace.

The siblings stayed close to the park that week, for that was where meals were served. They would watch their parents go about the tedious task of hunting for food, but hunting was not high on their agenda. They were happy to watch. There was a world out there and they wanted to know what was in it. Their parents might be happy, poking around for grubs all day, but they were not.

This is always a worrying time for parents, for this is when offspring can begin to mix with the wrong crowd, and Albert already had concerns about his daughter. Alice had an overly caring nature which gave her a tendency to mix with undesirables. She needed to change her ways, or she could become one of society's misfits.

A situation had already occurred. The siblings had been waiting for their breakfast one morning when Alice had looked up and noticed a cute little caterpillar crawling along a branch.

'Good morning,' she said.

'Good morning,' said the caterpillar.

'My name is Alice. What is yours?'

'Herbert.'

'What are you doing, Herbert?'

'I'm looking for food.'

'Oh, we don't have to worry about that. Our parents bring us our food.'

36

'You are so lucky,' said Herbert. 'I never knew my parents. They left me in an egg, stuck to a branch in this bush.'

Alice was not sure how to respond to such a sad story, and so she began one of her own.

'I am learning to fly,' she said.

'I am going to fly one day too,' said Herbert. 'I am going to grow wings and turn into a beautiful butterfly.'

Alice was delighted by the thought of her little friend becoming a beautiful butterfly.

'Oh, I can't wait to see that, Herbert. Please come and see me when you have your wings.'

'I will,' said Herbert, 'and I hope to see you flying soon as well.'

'Thank you,' said Alice. 'I know I will be flying soon, but it is much harder to fly than I thought.'

Alice watched Herbert as he inspected a leaf on the branch above her head. He was an orphan, abandoned at birth, yet he seemed so nice. *What an inspiring little gentleman*, she thought. *He should go far in life*.

Just then, Albert arrived. He spied Herbert and gulped him down. Alice was in shock.

'You just ate Herbert,' she screamed. She was inconsolable.

Albert turned to Max. 'What's up with your sister?'

'You just ate her friend.'

Albert frowned. 'You guys need to start learning more about your food. If it moves, you can eat it. Please pay more attention in class.'

That was the day Alice discovered that feelings of guilt can come from knowing what you eat, and the reason why mothers always tell their children, 'Never talk to your food.'

12

CHARLIE

Like all teenagers, the adolescent Magpies were ready to rebel, for their wings gave them freedom. Alice wanted to travel and see the world, while Max could not decide whether to be an adventurer or a detective. Their parent's boring routine of hunting for food and maintaining law and order did not impress them. Boring routine was not for them, and law and order stood in the way of good adventure.

It was in this frame of mind that the siblings pondered their future as they sat high in their old nest tree, looking down at their now abandoned nest.

'Can't believe we once all lived in that,' said Max.

'Gosh no, we must have been little then,' said Alice. 'Look at us now.'

With that, she preened a feather on her breast and then checked that all her other feathers were in place. Suddenly, they heard loud screeching and the same words being repeated over and over again.

'I am in here. I am in here.'

They had heard these cries many times before, but no one ever took notice of them. They wanted to investigate their cause, but they could not fly. But now they could fly, and Max was curious to find out more about the shouts.

'I'm wagging school,' he said. 'I'm off to be a detective and solve the mystery of that screeching. Are you coming, Sis?'

Alice had her doubts. 'Sounds like it might be dangerous, Maxie. I should stay here and tell our parents where you have gone. They can go and look for your body if you don't come back.'

Alice giggled at Max's frown.

Max left his sister and headed for the screeches. It sounded like a bird, but he did not know what type of bird, and he wondered how a bird could always be getting trapped in something.

The sound was coming from behind a house. Max landed on its roof. This was the first time that Max had stood on a roof, and he was curious to find out what it was made from. He pecked at it. It was hard, and it sounded hollow. He listened and could hear Humans moving about below. He had to be wary, for Brian's abduction still played on his mind.

Max looked around and discovered that there were houses everywhere. *So, this is what the rest of the world looks like,* he thought, and then he noticed that fences stood between the houses. Max guessed that Humans lived in the houses, but he could see no purpose for the fences. *How can Humans move about in a world full of fences?* he thought. He was glad that he was a bird and could simply fly over them. Then he heard more screeching, and he looked down. The noise was coming from a large, wooden box, that stood on four wooden legs.

It's a screeching box, thought Max.

The screeching came again. 'I am in here; I am in here.'

Max reviewed the evidence as a good detective should. *No, someone is screeching inside the box,* he concluded.

Max wondered what to do, and he chose the hero option. His instinct told him to be wary, but an adventurer has to be bold.

'Max to the rescue!' he squawked as he launched himself from the roof, landing just in front of the box. To his surprise, the front of the box was covered with wire netting, and through the wire Max could see a large, white bird.

'Hello there, young man, here to rescue someone?' the bird asked.

Max was surprised. The bird was speaking with a casual but gravelly voice, yet moments before, he had been screeching. Max stared at the bird and then remembered his manners. He gathered his thoughts.

'Hello, my name is Max, and I am a Magpie. What is your name?'

'My name is Charlie. I am a Sulphur Crested Cockatoo, and I can see that you are a Magpie.'

Max was puzzled. He thought that Charlie would be excited to see a rescuer, but he was acting all calm and polite.

'Why are you screeching and how did you get stuck in that box?' Max asked.

Charlie shrugged, as if Max was asking a silly question. 'I screech so that people will visit me. Screeching is what us Cockatoos do.'

'But how did you get stuck in a box?'

'This is not a box; this is my cage. I live here. I have always lived here. This is my home.'

'Really?' said Max. 'Have you never seen the world? My sister wants to see the world.'

Charlie paused and then looked Max in the eye. His expression darkened and he partly spread his wings. Max could sense that Charlie was about to say something profound.

'Tell her to be very careful. The world is an unfriendly place for birds such as us, but I am safe. Humans keep me protected in this cage.'

Charlie's warning surprised Max, for he thought that Humans were bad, and keeping someone in a cage seemed to support his argument. He decided to tell Charlie about Brian's abduction, and about his father declaring war on all Humans.

Charlie listened, and then thought how best to explain his point of view to his young sceptic. 'I am sorry to hear about your brother, young Magpie, but let me tell you a secret. It is a secret about Humans.' Charlie beckoned Max to come closer to the wire.

'What's the secret?' Max asked.

Charlie leaned forward on his perch and whispered, 'Birds make Humans happy, and if we are very clever, we can make them do whatever we want. Your brother is probably safe.'

'I hope so,' said Max, 'but I doubt that he could make a Human happy. He could never cheer us up.'

'Who knows?' said Charlie. 'Humans are strange creatures and strange things make them happy.'

Max did not wish to dwell further on Brian's fate. 'Do you like living in a cage?' he asked.

Charlie shrugged again. 'Why not? A Human visits me, he looks after me, and he feeds me.'

'What does he feed you?' Max asked.

Charlie flicked some seeds through the wire. Max sampled one, but it was not to his liking, and he gave his blunt assessment.

'My parents bring me food that is much better than that. If Humans were really nice people, they would bring you worms.'

Charlie was offended by Max's criticism. 'Your parents won't feed you forever,' he snapped.

'Really?' queried Max, as he wondered how Charlie could tell the future. Max thought that his parents would always feed him, but Charlie was telling him otherwise. How could Charlie know such a thing?

'One day, you will have to feed yourself,' Charlie went on, 'but if you make a Human happy, they sometimes give you food as well.'

'How do you make a Human happy when you are stuck in a cage?' Max asked, his detective mind seeking flaws in Charlie's story.

Charlie's eyes lit up, for Max was asking the question that always gave him pleasure to answer.

'I watch the Human's hand. If it moves from side to side or up and down, I sway my body and bob my head. Somehow, it makes the Human happy, and it makes him say, "Dance, Charlie, dance". I can make him say that any time I like.'

'You can make a Human say things?' Max asked.

'I can make a Human say anything,' Charlie replied. 'I listen to them say something, and if I feel like it, I say it back. Saying it back makes them say it again. I can make them say it all day if I want. Charlie wants a cracker, is a good one. I get food treats whenever I get them saying that.'

Max was confused. Were Humans good or bad people? His dad was saying one thing and Charlie was saying the other. Charlie seemed wise, but so did his dad. This was not going to be an easy case to solve. He needed to ask another question.

'Why is the world an unfriendly place?' he asked.

Charlie paused, and his mood became sombre as he recalled a frightening event. He told how a flock of Cockatoos sometimes flew over, all screeching at once. He would screech back, 'I am in here, I am in here'. Usually, they ignored his calls, but there was one time when they flew down for a visit. Sadly, they were not nice, and they poked fun at him for being stuck in his cage. He told them they were being mean, and he wished that he could fly free in the sky like them. With that, one undid the catch on his cage and the little door flew open. 'Come join us,' they all screeched.

Charlie broke briefly from his story. 'Cockatoos are very clever at undoing things you know.'

Max was suitably impressed.

Charlie went on. The Cockatoos continued screeching, 'Come out, come out,' and so Charlie did. They took off and so he followed, but they climbed high into the sky and Charlie's wings became too weak for him to keep up. He had to rest in a tree, and the flock flew away. That was when the nightmare began.

Noisy Miners attacked him, all screaming their frightening war cry. Some swooped at his head while others pulled at his feathers. He asked them to go away, but his attackers increased in number. He had to flee, but to where? He was confused and could not remember the way back to his cage. He took off, but his wings could not take him far. He crash landed in a thick bush and crawled to its centre. There he hid for a day and a half. Close by, he could hear the Miners daring him to come out. During the night, it rained, and he was cold and hungry. Next day, a Human found him. Somehow, the Human knew where his cage was and brought him back. He had not been out of his cage since.

Max was surprised that the Miners could frighten a large bird like Charlie, but he could see that the subject troubled him and so he asked no more questions. He had successfully solved the mystery of the screeching box, but he now had two new cases to solve. Were Humans good or bad people, and can birds really make Humans happy?

However, it was time for him to leave. He thanked Charlie for his stories, and Charlie thanked Max for his visit.

Max left, eager to tell Alice about his great, white guru, who lived in a box.

'Come again,' Charlie screeched as Max flew away.

'I will,' Max squawked, and as he headed for home, he heard the screeching begin again. 'I am in here. I am in here.' It was as if Charlie had already forgotten Max's visit.

13

DOPEY

Max was not the only one to wag school that morning. Alice decided that it was time for her to see the world, and she looked about for a high vantage point. The TV antenna that stood on top of a nearby house, looked ideal. She had often seen a Dove perched there.

Alice flew to the antenna and looked around. Alas, to her dismay, she discovered that the world was full of houses. There was the odd tall tree, but not enough to get a bird excited. However, when she looked in the direction to where the sun rose each morning, she saw a range of hills. The hills gave her a glimmer of hope, for the houses stopped where the hills began. The hills were pretty, a patchwork of blues, greens, and yellows, which was what she had hoped the whole world would look like. She stared at the hills and wondered what lay beyond, and then she looked back to the houses, and sighed.

As Alice sat, feeling glum about her surroundings, the Dove arrived on his usual morning rounds. He perched alongside her, but Alice was so preoccupied with her thoughts that she did not notice his arrival. His voice gave her a start.

'New in this part of the world, kid?'

Alice jumped, and then regained her composure.

'Yes, I am new. I hope you don't mind me sitting on your perch?'

'The more the merrier,' the Dove laughed. 'My name is Dopey, what's yours?'

'My name is Alice.' She paused, for a question came to mind, but she would have to ask it tactfully. 'Dopey is a very unusual name. Did your parents call you Dopey?'

'No, they called me Aloysius. Can you imagine, Aloysius Dove? No way. A good Human gave me the name, Dopey. Dopey the Dove just rolls off the tongue don't you think? The Human thinks that I don't know what it means, but who cares, I like it better than Aloysius.'

It was a long explanation for such a simple question. Alice wondered if Doves always gave long answers. She pondered the risk of asking another question, but Dopey kept the conversation going.

'It's a great spot up here, lots of nice breeze, and I really appreciate you coming along to help.'

Alice could see nothing great at all, and the breeze was certainly not special. It was the same breeze that she could find anywhere, and nothing was going to make the houses disappear. However, she did not wish to be a killjoy.

'I like the breeze, but the view is a little disappointing,' she said.

Dopey chuckled. 'The view, who cares about the view? I think it is great that you are here to help.'

'Help?' queried Alice.

Dopey winked. 'Check below.'

Alice looked down. There was a large, whitish patch, just below where they were perched. 'Is that what I think it is?' she asked, slightly shocked.

'Sure is. Great bomb target don't you think? I come here every morning, take in the breeze and drop a couple of messages on this house. Some might call me Dopey, but I get the last laugh. With your help, the two of us can drop an even bigger message.'

It was another long answer, and the conversation was becoming a little indelicate. Alice was cautious of Dopey and his odd behaviour, but it did have its funny side. Dopey seemed that he could be fun, but she wondered why he had chosen that particular house.

'Why do you choose this house when there are so many houses to choose from?' she asked, hoping that the answer would be funny, but Dopey became serious.

'We are sitting on the TV antenna of Slingshot Sam,' he said. 'He is the boy who once terrorised all the Doves in the district. Fortunately, his parents have taken his slingshot away, but if you ever see a boy with something in his hands, and he suddenly looks straight at you, fly away because it might be Slingshot Sam. If you don't, he will fire a stone, and you will be dead.'

'We should warn everybody,' Alice said in alarm.

'I tried once,' said Dopey, 'but it's hard to convince people when your name is Dopey. I stopped warning them long ago because they said I was an idiot.'

'I believe you,' said Alice, 'and I won't tell anyone either, because I don't want people calling me an idiot.' Alice looked down again and changed the subject. 'You have certainly made a nice pile,' she complimented.

'Oh, it is not all my work,' Dopey confessed. 'Others chip in as well. Please feel free to help because the rain washes it away.'

'Where does it go?'

Alice's question brought a gleam to Dopey's eye. His grave tone disappeared as he pointed towards a large, cylindrical object, and then he explained the workings and purpose of a rainwater tank. It was a simple set up that Humans use to catch water from the roof. Dopey explained how the Humans drank the water, and he mused how they never took notice of what might be floating in what they drank.

'It is my gift that just keeps giving,' he chuckled.

'You are evil,' Alice giggled.

'I know,' laughed Dopey.

Alice was curious to know more about Dopey's good Human, and so Dopey began another long story. He told how he had been sitting on a lawn behind a house when a Falcon swooped and attacked him. Luckily, he managed to scramble behind a large pot, but the Falcon waited, knowing that Dopey could not stay there long because the sun's rays were burning down on him. However, the Human who lived in the house saw what had happened and came to his rescue. The Human chased the Falcon away, but Dopey was too frightened to come out in case the Falcon came back. The Human realised this and put an umbrella beside the pot to make shade. Next, he pushed a bowl of water behind the pot, together with some nice food. After that, he went away.

Dopey told how he had stayed behind the pot all day, not knowing the whereabouts of the Falcon. He left about dark. Next day, he returned to the house and the Human came out to see him. The Human threw him some food. After that, Dopey visited the Human every day and they became friends. He would eat food from the Human's hand, and the Human began to call him Dopey. The Human would come out of his house and shout his name. Dopey said that he did not mind being called Dopey, because it meant that he was about to be fed.

Then Dopey made a suggestion that would have horrified Alice's parents. Albert's fears about his daughter mixing with the wrong crowd were about to come true.

'I should take you to visit my Human friend,' said Dopey. 'I am sure he would give you treats, but you must promise me one thing.'

'What's that?' Alice asked.

'You must never visit my friend in the afternoon.'

It seemed an odd request, but Dopey was an odd bird. However, it would be an easy promise to keep. Morning visits sounded fine.

'I promise,' said Alice, and then she remembered her yearning to see the world. 'Tell me, is there anyone around here who knows about the world? I want to learn all about the world.'

Dopey thought for a moment. 'You need to find Nebby. He's our authority on science and other matters. He also hears all the gossip, but he can be hard to find, for he lives in whatever tree he thinks is his favourite, but no tree stays his favourite for long.'

'Does he fly from tree to tree?' Alice asked.

Dopey laughed. 'No, not Nebby, but you will see why when you meet him.'

'Should I introduce myself as a friend of Dopey?'

Dopey frowned. 'No, he knows me as the Pigeon.'

'Is that so bad?' giggled Alice. 'It sounds a nicer name than Dopey.'

Alice had forgotten her manners and had accidentally expressed an opinion on the subject she had been trying hard to avoid.

Dopey raised his voice. 'Pigeons are stupid birds,' he said. 'Haven't you seen how a Pigeon walks? Neck in, neck out, neck in, neck out. It makes you queasy just watching them, and not only that, they live in cages. The Humans kick them out of their cages and take them far beyond the far beyond, just to get rid of them, and what do they do? They fly all the way back so that they can be locked in their cages again.'

'I'm sorry,' said Alice. 'I've never met a Pigeon.'

'Apology accepted,' said Dopey. 'Tomorrow, I will take you to meet my good Human.'

'Ok,' said Alice. 'That sounds like a date.'

Dopey winked. 'See ya tomorrow, kid,' he said, and then he flew away.

I guess he has important Dove matters to attend to, Alice thought, wistfully.

14

THE MARTIAL ARTS

That afternoon, the siblings found themselves in trouble for wagging school. Albert demanded to know where they had been, and Alice was happy to oblige. She thought that her dad would approve of her new friend because Dopey waged a vendetta against a bad Human. He was the type of boy she could safely bring home. But alas, she was mistaken, for her dad flew into a rage.

'You will never talk to the Pigeon again,' he squawked.

Alice was surprised to hear that her dad knew that Dopey was sometimes called the Pigeon. Her dad obviously knew Dopey or knew of him. With a lack of judgement that is common in the adolescent years, she answered, 'His name is not Pigeon. He hates that name, and if you must know, his real name is Aloysius.'

Alice's defiance did not go unrewarded. Albert squawked louder.

'That boy is an idiot. The name Dopey says it all.'

Alice was a pleasant girl by nature, but she had a fiery Magpie heart. Her dad was wrong, and she was right. He had no right to talk about Dopey that way. She squawked back, 'Dopey is very smart. He knows how to deal with the bad Humans, and he makes friends with the good ones. Dopey is going to take me to meet a good Human.'

Alice had spoken her piece, and it was all too much for Albert. He screamed in her face. 'You will never go anywhere with that bird, never, never, never.' He was repeating himself, and everyone knew what that meant.

Max tried to calm things. 'Alice is right. I have been talking to my new friend, Charlie. He says that if we make friends with the Humans, they will give us food.'

Albert turned to Max but then hesitated. He had to compose himself, for he could feel his body begin to tremble, and trembling was a sign of weakness. After several deep breaths, he regained composure and began speaking quietly, but his quieter voice sounded even more threatening.

'That's all I need, you talking to the crazy Cockatoo. Read my beak. The Humans are not our friends, and we never take food from them, never, never, never.'

He was repeating again. It was time for everyone to back away.

There was silence for a short while. Albert meandered around, angrily pecking at various objects on the ground, while Alice and Max stood frozen, too frightened to move. Then Albert called the class to order. 'Time for your next lesson,' he squawked.

More lessons, thought Max. *How come we are having more lessons? We already know everything.* But the teacher's voice sounded sinister.

'Today, you will learn about the Martial Arts,' he squawked, 'and it is a lesson I am going to enjoy teaching.' With that, he rushed at Alice, pushing her onto her back. 'Defend yourself, defend yourself, or I will peck your eyes out.'

Albert held Alice down and thrust his deformed beak at her head. He had one claw held to her throat while the other pinned her outstretched wing to the ground. Instinctively, Alice pointed her beak at Albert's head, making her eyes a difficult target to reach. After several thrusts, Albert got past her beak and struck Alice in the forehead. She opened her beak, using it as a shield. Her attacker then tried to peck around the open beak but failed to inflict a second blow. He stepped back.

Alice rolled upright and squatted. She dared not move for fear that her father might attack again. She was in shock, and her tail quivered. Muriel was standing close by.

'That was far too violent for a first lesson,' she squawked.

'Keep out of this,' growled Albert. 'The girl needs to be kept in line.'

Albert turned to Max, but Max was ready. He rolled onto his back just as his father lunged, and he pushed Albert off with his legs. Albert lunged again. This time, Max opened his beak as a shield, the same as he had seen Alice do.

Albert broke off the attack. 'That is how Magpies practice their Martial Arts,' he squawked. 'Every Magpie must know how to defend and how to attack. If you want to live a life of peace, you must know the art of war. Just ask a Noisy Miner. No one messes with a Magpie. You will now fight each other, and next time I test you, I will not be so merciful.'

Albert retreated to his throne to watch the gladiatorial conquest, while Muriel stayed ringside where she could intervene if necessary.

The siblings faced each other. Max was ready, but Alice was wondering what her father meant by, 'Not so merciful next time'. Had it not been for his deformed beak, she might have lost an eye.

Max winked. 'Better make this look good for the old bloke,' he said in their silent language, and then he rushed at her with his wings partly spread. He was trying to look menacing, and Alice reeled back as he landed on top of her. She put up little resistance, and he pinned her to the ground. 'Pathetic effort,' he laughed. 'You fight like a girl.'

'Like a girl!' squawked Alice, and then she planted her claws firmly into Max's chest. With a mighty push, he went flying. He landed on his back, and before he could move, she was on top of him.

'Like a girl!' Alice squawked again. 'Give in. Give in.'

Max lay stunned, for Alice had him in the same grip that Albert had used on her. Their mother stepped in.

'Alice is the winner.'

'She took me by surprise,' Max protested.

'Like a girl,' taunted Alice.

'I think that is enough fighting for now,' declared Muriel. 'You can have your rematch later.'

Shortly thereafter, the siblings discussed how best to deal with the Martial Arts classes. Max had a suggestion.

'We need to take it in turns of winning. That way, Dad can't pick on us. It's my turn to win next.'

Alice laughed. 'Not a problem, Maxie. That is, provided you don't bring up this fighting like a girl business again. You do, and you will lose every time.'

15

THE CRAZIES

Alice broke her date with Dopey the next day, for she did not want a repeat of her father's wrath. Instead, she decided to look for Nebby and Max joined her. However, Nebby was a person who moved from tree to tree, and they soon found that a bird with no fixed address was hard to find. Alice asked a Noisy Miner if he knew the whereabouts of Nebby.

'I wouldn't tell you if I did,' came the reply.

The Miners had driven most of the birds out of Gum Tree Park, and those that remained avoided conflict with the Miners by hiding from them. This made it difficult for the siblings to find anyone who could help with their Nebby hunt. They knew there were other birds about, for someone was committing acts of vandalism to upset the Humans. They would scatter leaf litter onto places where the Humans did not want leaf litter to be. The Humans would then sweep the litter away only to find it back again the next day. Dopey was not the only one waging a vendetta against Humans.

There was also a bird that whistled through the night, keeping everyone awake. Max called him the Party Bird, and Alice called him the Insomniac. Also, they had heard a warrior who defied the Miners at dusk. The Miners would shriek their war cry from the treetops, warning other birds to roost elsewhere. Between their screeches, a shrill cry would come from the ground. The lone warrior would be shouting, 'I am going nowhere.'

The siblings guessed that one of these birds must be Nebby, but which one?

They looked in every tree but found nobody. Then they heard a distant cry. The warrior, who defied the Miners, was shouting at someone. They flew towards the cries, and as they got closer, the words became clearer.

'Get out of here, and take that, and that, and that.'

A cautious approach was needed because loud thumps and crashes accompanied the shouts of the warrior. These were the sounds of battle, but the warrior's foe remained silent.

They landed on top of a pole from which they could see down a road. Not far along was an angry bird, a mini-Magpie. This little man was attacking an innocent motor car. For some reason, this immobile object had infuriated him. With ruffled feathers, he repeatedly rushed at it, striking it with his beak and scratching it with his claws. His attacks were ferocious, and he knew how to fight. However, he appeared to show poor judgement in choosing an opponent.

Alice turned to Max. 'What on earth is he wild about?'

Max was equally bemused. 'Don't know,' he replied. 'That car must have done something to upset him.'

'Better make sure that you never upset him,' quipped Alice.

Alice regarded her brother as having poor social skills. He could be insensitive and upset people without realising it, and she did not want him upsetting this little chap.

They watched the little man as he continued his attack. At times, he would rest to catch his breath, and then he would attack again.

'Get out of here. Get out of here. This place is not big enough for the two of us.' But the car would not move, and so the little man would attack again.

CLUNK!

Still the car remained motionless. Another attack was needed.

CLUNK!

'What does he mean, "the two of us"?' said Max. 'I can only see one of him, unless he thinks they are both cars.'

'Bit of a size difference,' laughed Alice.

'I am never going to pick on him,' said Max. 'He wants to fight anything that moves.'

'I think that's the problem,' Alice giggled. 'That car won't move, and he wants it gone.'

'Those things only move when they have Humans inside of them,' Max chuckled. 'At least we know why he yells at the Miners to be quiet. With all that clunking, he must get horrible headaches.'

'Let's go,' said Alice. 'If that person is Nebby, then I won't be visiting him. I am not that anxious to learn about the world and hear all the gossip.'

Just then, they heard another call. It was the Party Bird, and it came from the direction of the creek. The bird sounded jolly, but someone was frustrating him. 'Fly straight you cheat; you can't get away. Stop that flitting about you maniac,' the bird was saying.

'That bird never sleeps,' growled Alice. 'I need to speak to him. Someone has to tell him that he keeps the neighbourhood awake.'

'Better see how big he is first,' cautioned Max. 'Besides, he doesn't keep me awake.'

'Nothing keeps you awake,' quipped Alice. 'Sometimes, I think you are asleep even when you have your eyes open.'

They flew to a tree from where they could see what was happening. The Party Bird was chasing a butterfly, and he was black and white, the same as the midget Magpie, only smaller. He had a predominantly long tail that gave him excellent manoeuvrability in the air, but he could not catch the butterfly he was chasing. Alice reminisced for a moment.

'I wonder if that butterfly is related to Herbert. Poor Herbert, he never got to be a butterfly.'

But Max was more concerned about the Party Bird's colour.

'Doesn't it worry you, Sis, that all the black and white birds we come across seem a little crazy?'

'Your point being?' Alice responded.

'Nothing.' Max knew better than to debate an issue with his sister. 'I guess us Magpies can be the exception,' he mumbled.

The butterfly continued his erratic flight, easily avoiding his pursuer whose twists and turns in the air were proving futile. Finally, the butterfly took refuge in a bush, and so the bird rested on the ground, waiting for the butterfly's next move. Alice yelled to the bird.

'Hey, bird, do you know if Nebby lives around here?'

'Darn girls,' Max muttered. 'They always ask for directions. They have no spirit of adventure.'

The Party Bird looked up and pointed. 'He's over in that tree.'

As he spoke, the butterfly flew out of the bush. With a shout of 'Yikes, yikes, and tallyho,' the Party Bird was off again.

Alice looked towards the tree where the bird had pointed. 'I guess he meant the tree over there,' she said, 'but I don't see anyone in it.'

They flew to the tree and found it devoid of birds. They listened but could only hear the shouts of the mini-Magpie and the cries of yikes and tallyho. Max was ready to give up on Alice's Nebby hunt.

'I think your Nebby is a stupid bird that Dopey made up,' he said. 'Only a bird with a stupid name like Dopey would give another bird a stupid name like Nebby. If Nebby really does exist, then he probably moves from place to place because nobody likes him.'

Max felt better for having said all that, but Alice was disappointed in her brother's sudden loss of commitment to her project. 'We must keep looking,' she pleaded. 'Dopey said that Nebby can tell us about the world, and he knows all the gossip.'

Max laughed. 'I think Dad was right. Anyone recommended by someone with a name like Dopey, is bound to be a nut case.'

Alice began thinking evil thoughts about her brother. She had never seen a Magpie practice their martial arts in a tree, but she was about to give it a try. Max was pushing her to the limit.

'Come on out, Nebby, wherever you are,' squawked Max. 'I want to see what someone with a stupid name like Nebby, looks like.'

'I can hear you.'

The quiet little voice startled them. They jumped and looked around. Huddled next to the trunk of the tree was a furry object. Alice hopped over to inspect it. The object smelt like an animal that had been rolling in eucalyptus leaves, but it did not move. She thought about pecking it but decided to try another investigative method first. She asked it a question.

'Did you just speak?'

The question worked, for the furry object moved; that is to say, a single eye opened and peered at her. Alice waited as the eye performed a slow examination of its intruder. Moments passed, but still no answer came. She asked another question.

'What are you doing?'

The eye closed. It appeared that Max had woken the animal. Alice was about to scold Max for his insensitive remarks when the animal spoke once more.

'I am thinking. That is what I do. I sit here and think.'

'Is that all you do all day, just think?' Max asked.

'Oh no,' said the animal. 'I listen as well. I hear all the gossip because everyone thinks I'm asleep. Sometimes, I even hear unflattering things about myself.'

Alice gave Max her hardest frown and then the animal continued talking in a soft voice.

'Don't worry, young Magpies, I was a young Koala myself once, and I know your dad. We sometimes hang out together in his man tree. Sad man, your dad. He has the weight of the world on his shoulders.'

'Are you Nebby?' asked Alice.

The animal opened both eyes and looked at her. 'I am, and you would be the Alice and Max the Pigeon has told me about.'

'We are,' said Alice, 'but Dopey hates being called that name.'

Nebby sank his head into his chest, as if ashamed. Alice heard a muffled chuckle, and then another. Then Nebby looked up at her and smiled. 'I know,' he said, and then he chuckled some more.

Nebby had a wry sense of humour.

16

NEBBY

Alice enjoyed her first visit with Nebby, but she was annoyed with Max because he hogged most of Nebby's attention. At first, they watched the Party Bird as he chased the clumsy butterfly.

Max made an astute observation. 'That bird is a brilliant flyer. He can twist and turn because of his long tail, but look at that ridiculous butterfly. He is a hopeless flyer because he has no tail. He has no idea where he is going. He just flops around in the air until he lands on something. Why would Mother Nature bother to make a flying creature and not give it a tail?'

Max expected everyone to agree, but Nebby frowned. Max had dared to question the wisdom of Mother Nature. 'Isn't it funny how the clever bird can never catch the clumsy flyer?' Nebby said. 'It makes you wonder whose side Mother Nature is on.'

Max pondered Nebby's cryptic answer and decided it best that he keep his opinions to himself in future. 'Who is that black and white bird?' he asked.

They waited for Nebby to reply, but Nebby was not a man of sudden action. He did everything at a leisurely pace. So far, he had opened his eyes once, closed them once, scratched himself twice, looked around twice, but nothing else, and the spacing of his words complemented his almost motionless body. Following a brief period of nothing happening, he answered, 'The black and white bird is Willy, the Willy Wagtail, and Willy is fearless. I have seen him hunt insects that fly from the ground to escape the Human's machine as it chops the grass on Gum Tree Park. He swoops in front of the machine as it comes towards him, and he shows no fear. The Noisy Miners have all seen his bravery, and they leave him alone.'

In the distance, they heard once more the shouts of the fighting man who was attacking the motor car. Max asked who he was, and

Nebby chuckled. 'The fighting man is Murray, the Murray Magpie. Murray is a fearless guardian of his territory, and like Willy, the Noisy Miners give him no trouble.'

'What possible problem could he have with a car?' Max asked.

Nebby chuckled again. 'The problem with my friend Murray, is that he does not understand the science of reflection. The car has shiny parts in which Murray sees a reflection of himself, but he thinks it is another Murray Magpie trespassing in his territory. He tells the other bird to go, but the other bird stays. A fight always follows, but every time Murray strikes at the other bird, something hard and invisible gets in the way. It drives him mad.'

It had taken some time for Nebby to give his answers and Alice was becoming impatient. Nebby was answering Max's questions even though Max had come with no questions to ask. Meanwhile, her questions about the world remained. Max was about to comment that perhaps Murray did not like the look of the chap he thought he was fighting, but he was cut short when Alice almost bumped him off the branch.

'Careful, Sis, I nearly had an accident,' said Max.

Alice frowned. 'It would not have been an accident. You are wasting Nebby's time when we have important things to ask.'

Alice looked across at Nebby, feeling embarrassed that he had just witnessed how a sister sometimes has to deal with an annoying brother, but Nebby's eyes were closed. *Surely, he is not going to sleep again,* she thought.

'Excuse me, Mister Nebby, I have come to ask you about the world. They say that you know all about the world.'

Nebby opened his eyes, stretched a little, and then looked at Alice. 'What would you like to know about the world?' he said, and then he yawned.

Nebby appeared exhausted after answering Max's questions, so Alice decided to ask her most important question first. 'How big is the world?' she asked.

Nebby paused; his eyelids flickered. *Oh no, please don't go to sleep*, thought Alice, but then Nebby answered. 'A very good question, my girl, but no one knows how big the world is because no one has ever seen where it ends. A Mutton Bird once told a Sea Gull, and the Sea Gull told a Crow, and the Crow told me, that Mutton Birds fly from one side of the world to the other, but they have never seen where it ends. They just finish up back where they started.'

'How can that be?' asked Max, butting in again.

'I don't know,' said Nebby. 'I sit here and think about it, but the answer has yet to come to me. But don't worry, science will solve the mystery one day.'

'Has anyone seen the end of the world?' Alice asked.

Nebby paused for a while and then answered, 'The Penguins tell the Mutton Birds that the end of the world cannot be reached because it lies beyond their land of frozen water.'

'Who are the Penguins?' asked Max, whose detective mind was probing for flaws in Nebby's answers.

Alice rolled her eyes. She was becoming annoyed at her brother, for he was monopolizing the visit. *Next time I come, Max is staying home,* she thought.

However, Nebby remained patient and answered the question. 'Penguins come from a land of frozen water. They are birds that cannot fly because their wings are tiny, but they use their tiny wings to swim through water as if they are fish.'

'That sounds ridiculous,' said Max, forgetting that he had resolved to keep his opinions to himself. 'I am going to be a detective one day, and a good detective would never believe that story.'

It was now difficult to tell whom out of Alice and Nebby was getting the more annoyed with Max. 'You only think it is not true because you are not a scientist,' Nebby growled. 'We scientists understand these things, but sceptics like you will go through life knowing nothing. I suggest that you think more about science and less about being a detective.'

Alice was amused to see that Max had gotten himself into trouble once more. Her brother needed to improve his manners, and Nebby might be the one who could teach him. Nebby was knowledgeable and knew about Sea Gulls, Mutton Birds, and Penguins. There were so many different types of birds in the world, and they all knew different things.

'Where can I meet birds who can tell me more about the world?' Alice asked.

Nebby slowly raised his arm and pointed towards the hills. 'Beyond those hills lies the Great River. It is the meeting place of birds from many places. They go there to share wisdom and knowledge.'

'Have you ever been there?' asked Alice, excited that such a place existed.

Nebby shook his head. 'No, it is too far away. I once met a Crow who said he had been there, but it would be too far for a Magpie to fly.'

If a Crow can get there, I can get there, Alice thought to herself. A place of wisdom and knowledge was worth a long journey. However, it was time to go because Nebby was losing patience with Max.

'Come on, Maxie,' she said, 'our parents will be wondering where we are, and you know what happened last time.' She looked at Nebby. 'Can we come back and ask more questions. I want to know more about the Great River?'

Nebby smiled. 'Any time, and hopefully, the two of us can teach your brother some manners at the same time.'

With that, Nebby closed his eyes and began to snore.

17

DARE DEVIL DOPEY

Next morning, Alice slipped away from home to look for Dopey, and she found him basking in the sun. *That Dopey is a very strange bird,* she thought. It was a hot day, and most creatures were looking for shade, but there was Dopey, sprawled out on hot paving.

Alice decided to show off her Magpie skills and aimed directly at him. She plunged downward, pulling out of her dive just before impact. With a magnificent swoop, she landed close enough to peck Dopey on the beak. He did not flinch.

'What do you think of that?' Alice asked as she proudly folded her wings to her side.

'Wasn't looking, I have to keep an eye on that cat.'

Alice looked across to a tall, green rubbish bin. Crouched beside it was Felix, his body rigid, his eyes fixed on them both.

'We are in danger, get out of here,' Alice squawked in panic.

'No, it's a game.'

Dopey appeared to be enjoying Felix's attention. He got up and slowly meandered towards the green bin. Then he stopped, almost within a cat's striking distance. Next, he turned his back on Felix. Alice thought that she was seeing the reason why they called him Dopey.

'Get out of there,' she cried.

'Don't worry, I'm playing tease the cat,' Dopey laughed. 'He wants me to face him. That way, he can catch me as I take off. But with my back turned, I take off flying away from him, and he knows that he can't catch up.'

'Slow coach,' Dopey taunted.

Felix did not move.

'That sounds good in theory, but don't push your luck,' cautioned Alice.

'Done it many times,' Dopey replied. 'It drives him mad.'

Felix remained frozen.

Alice had seen enough, and she found a safe vantage point in the branches of a tall tree growing close by. Dopey flew up and perched beside her. He could play that game any time. He wanted to talk to Alice.

Felix grumbled and walked away. Getting Dopey was on his bucket list, and he was a patient cat. It had not happened that day, but Dopey's days were numbered.

Dopey was a confident Dove, and he liked impressing the girls. The fact that Alice was not a Dove did not bother him at all. He was happy showing off to any girl who took notice. He looked at Alice. 'What was that question you asked me before? It had something to do with something you did as you arrived?'

Alice felt indignant. 'My fantastic Magpie swoop. Don't you wish that Doves could swoop like Magpies?'

Dopey frowned. The question offended him. Alice wondered how a person called Dopey could be offended. Was she seeing his sensitive side?

'Watch this,' said Dopey.

He sprung from his branch and flew high into the air, his wings flapping. Once high above, he stalled, held his wings outright, and then turned towards the ground. Half gliding, half diving, he swooped back to the tree.

'That is how I do my Dove Dive,' he puffed. 'Doves are excellent flyers, all except Uncle Fred, that is.'

Dopey was panting.

'Who's Uncle Fred?' asked Alice.

Dopey regained his breath. 'Uncle Fred was our family's worst ever flyer. One windy day, he flew straight into a tree.' Dopey sounded sad as he talked about his Uncle Fred.

'What happened to him?' asked Alice.

Dopey continued. 'I flew over and found Uncle Fred asleep under the tree, and I could not wake him.'

'What did you do?'

Dopey sounded a little sadder. 'I came back the next day and found Uncle Fred, still asleep, covered with ants. I thought this rather strange because Uncle Fred hated ants.'

'What then?'

'I came back some time later, but Uncle Fred was gone. I guessed that the ants had taken him somewhere.'

Alice felt guilty that her question had caused Dopey to feel sad as she never wanted to make anyone feel sad. Action was needed to brighten things up. 'Let me see if I can do a Dove Dive,' she said.

Alice flew high into the air, higher than she had ever flown before. She hovered and looked down. Far below, Dopey was looking up from the tree.

'Go on, dive,' he called.

Suddenly, Alice thought more seriously about things. *I don't think Magpies are supposed to do this. We swoop from poles and trees. We don't dive from great heights, out of thin air. I think I should just stick to doing Magpie things.*

'Scaredy-cat girl,' shouted Dopey.

That taunt made the difference. Scaredy-cat and girl in the one sentence was a turning point in Alice's life. That was the moment when a sensitive young girl discovered her warrior queen within.

Alice dipped her head, held her wings out rigid, and began the longest downward swoop in Magpie history. Magpie history is probably an exaggeration, but that is how Alice would always tell the story.

Alice was well into her dive when she noticed a worrying development. The further she went, the faster she got. The tree was getting closer. She had never done this before. She had never flown this fast before. She thought about the demise of Uncle Fred and changed her plan.

'You are supposed to be landing in this tree,' Dopey shouted as she whizzed past. But Alice was going too fast to land anywhere. She had to slow down before reaching the ground, and so she spiralled to slow her speed. The spiral worked, and was a spectacular finish to her dive, which she followed up with a traditional, Magpie swoop landing.

'Harder than you thought,' Dopey yelled.

Alice flew back to him, her heart pounding. 'I don't think I should try landing in a tree,' she said, 'but the dive was so much fun. I am going to do it again.'

Alice had discovered the joy of the Dove Dive, a delight that Magpies did not indulge in. From that day on, she would do a Dove Dive whenever her spirits needed a lift.

She was about to try another Dove Dive when the Human came out of a house next to the tree. Dopey's eyes lit up. 'That's my good Human,' he said.

The Human looked up at the tree and called, 'Dopey,' and then he held out his hand in which there was food.

Dopey flew to the ground as Alice watched from the tree. She saw him peck the food from the outstretched hand. Then Dopey looked up to Alice. 'Come on down, he won't bite you.'

Alice was not so sure.

'Scaredy-cat,' Dopey teased.

Scaredy-cat, the challenge Alice could not resist. *I will show him*, she thought. She flew down and landed a safe distance away. The Human looked at her and then back at Dopey. 'You've brought a friend,' he said.

The Human flicked some food towards Alice, and she walked over and inspected the offering. It looked interesting, unlike anything that she had ever eaten. She tasted it. It was nice.

'If you want more, you will have to come closer,' said the Human in a firm but non-threatening tone.

He flicked some more food and it landed just beyond the reach of his arm. Alice approached with caution, one eye on the food and the other on the Human. She grabbed the food and stepped back. The Human did not move.

'Want some more?' he asked and flicked another bit to the same place. Alice stepped forward and ate, this time standing her ground.

The Human then looked away, but had his hand stretched out to her. In it was more food. He was daring Alice to take the food while he was not looking. Dopey was standing a short distance away.

'Go on, scaredy-cat, take it.'

Those magic words worked again. Alice grabbed the food and stepped back. The Human felt the slight tap of her beak. He put some more food in his hand, held it out, and looked away once more. Alice took the second offering.

By the end of the visit, Alice was taking food from the Human's hand, and he did not have to look away. Somehow, the bolder she became, the happier he appeared to be. She suggested to Dopey that they meet in the good Human's tree every day and visit him together.

Dopey agreed. 'Good idea. We will call the tree our meeting tree,' but then he cautioned, 'You must never come here in the afternoon.'

'Okay,' said Alice, not understanding the reason for the caution, which Dopey had now made for a second time, but she was happy to let Dopey make the rule.

That afternoon, Alice told Max about her visit to see Dopey's good Human. Max was fascinated to hear how she had made the Human happy, just like Charlie had said. However, he still shared his father's doubts about Dopey. He worried that Dopey was daring Alice to take risks, and he reminded her on the number one rule for survival—Never take an unnecessary risk.

Alice laughed. 'You will never be an adventurer if you never take a risk, Maxie.'

Max had no answer. *Why is it so difficult to argue with a girl?* he thought. He had often heard his father say that arguing with the fairer sex was futile, and he was beginning to agree. However, when Albert confronted his daughter later that day, he was in no mood to argue. He had heard gossip that Alice had taken food from a Human. He confronted her with her crime and discovered that she was proud of what she had done.

'So what,' she said. 'Humans don't want to hurt us. We make them happy.'

'Tell that to Brian you stupid girl,' Albert squawked in fury.

But Alice could see no reason to bring Brian into the conversation. Brian had brought his problems on himself.

'The Human likes to feed Dopey and me, and I intend going back,' she said.

Albert's efforts to straighten out his defiant daughter were proving futile, and if it were possible for a Magpie's face to turn red, his would have. 'Magpies never, never, never, take food from Humans,' he squawked. 'It shows a complete lack of self-respect. You will never, never, never, go to that Human's house again, and you will never, never, never, see Dopey again.'

Albert was repeating himself more times than ever before, and there was no need for Nebby to spread gossip about his rant. The whole neighbourhood was hearing it firsthand.

Albert flew to his man tree, leaving Alice to repent for her sins. She looked at Max.

'I guess that is as angry as he can get, and I survived. He can't stop me from seeing Dopey. He is just going to have to get used to it.'

'Let's hope he does,' said Max, but he had a feeling that the issue was far from settled.

18

THE WORLD

Alice yearned to get out and see the world, but Max was not interested. Charlie had told him that the world was an unfriendly place, and Max was happy to stay at home. This annoyed Alice, and she reminded Max that he would never become an adventurer if he never went anywhere.

Why do boys take so long to grow up? she would ask herself, for something inside told her that it was important for Max to learn about the world. This meant that he would have to go with her whenever she visited Nebby, but she would make a rule. Max was to ask no more questions, for his questions just wasted Nebby's time.

Next day, they visited Nebby again. He was easy to find this time, for he was still in the exact same place where they had left him. They perched in his tree.

'Time to practice my Magpie warble,' Alice announced.

She began to warble the loudest warble she could warble. Nebby stirred. She warbled some more. Alice watched the motionless Nebby, hoping to see a peeping eye. Nothing. She warbled again, and then came a slow, quiet voice. 'How can a Koala think with all that noise going on?'

'It's not noise, it's warbling. It's what us kings of the bush do,' Alice quipped.

Alice was being chipper. She thought that chipper was the best way to wake a sleeping person.

'Go away and be a king somewhere else,' Nebby mumbled. Being woken by someone being chipper did not impress him, but Alice was not daunted.

'But we have questions, and only the wise Nebby can answer them. Please answer our questions, Nebby.'

Alice's mum had told her that flattery was the best way to get the assistance of a male, and her mum was right. Nebby opened his eyes.

'I wasn't asleep you know, just thinking.'

'I know,' said Alice, not wishing to contradict, 'and we are here to find out more about the Great River.'

Nebby paused, as if reaching into his encyclopaedic brain to find the appropriate volume. Then he spoke. 'Only the legendary Great Gandor can tell you about the Great River, for only the Great Gandor sees all.'

Nebby's answer sounded wise, but not very helpful. *Who is the Great Gandor?* Alice wondered, *Great River, Great Gandor; why is everything great?* 'Are the Great Gandor and the Great River related?' she asked.

'Silly question,' said Nebby, and then he thought a little. 'The Great River is called the Great River because it is the great river, and the Great Gandor is called the Great Gandor because he sees all. I thought that would be perfectly clear.'

Alice was none the wiser. 'Just checking,' she said. 'So, if I want to find out more about the Great River, then I have to find the Great Gandor first?'

'Correct,' said Nebby, 'but I give you as much chance of getting an audience with the Great Gandor as did the Sparrows.'

'Who are the Sparrows?' asked Max.

Alice gave him a cold stare. That was his first warning, but Nebby was happy to answer Max's question.

Nebby told them the sad story of the Sparrows, who liked living in places where Humans lived. These harmless little birds spread cheer, for they would chirp the day away. However, their bodies were brown and devoid of colourful features, and so people took them for granted. When the Noisy Miners arrived, they drove the little Sparrows away, but it took some time for the Humans to realise that they were gone. Now, everyone misses them.

'Did they go to see the Great Gandor?' Alice asked.

Nebby's expression remained sad. 'Some say they did, but I hope not, because the Great Gandor eats those who visit him. My guess is that they found somewhere else to live. The world is a very big place.'

Max wondered about the Sparrows living in places where Humans lived. 'Are Humans good or bad people?' he asked. Alice pecked him in the ribs. That was his second warning.

Nebby smiled, and for the first time, he answered without hesitation. 'Humans love me,' he said. 'I can sit in my tree doing nothing, and Humans will look up and say how wonderful I am. The Humans think I am special.'

Nebby continued to smile as he thought about his popularity, and then he yawned, and then his head fell to his chest. It was time to leave.

Alice pondered on their visit as they flew back home. What had they learnt? She knew no more about the Great River than before. It appeared that only the Great Gandor knew about the Great River, and that he ate his visitors. She wondered what Max had learnt from the visit.

'Did you learn anything from today?' she asked.

'Sure did,' said Max. 'I learnt that everyone loves Nebby.'

Alice wondered why she had bothered to ask her brother, for she knew the type of answer he would give.

'I think I would like to meet the Great Gandor,' she said. 'He could answer all my questions.'

'Not if he eats you first,' laughed Max.

Alice frowned. 'That is your problem, adventure boy. You never want to take a risk.'

19

CROSSING THE LINE

As time went by, the sun grew warmer, and the days grew longer. Grubs became harder to find, but the siblings were now good hunters. They still pestered their parents for food, but their begging was mostly ignored. Alice had told Max about the meeting tree, and they would sneak away together and wait for the good Human to bring out food. Alice would take the food from the Human's hand, but Max was always cautious. At times, Alice practiced her Dove Dive, which everyone thought strange, but she only did it when her father was not about.

The family had settled into a new routine. The parents were at last relieved from the burden of child rearing, while their offspring enjoyed the freedom that comes with being a growing adult. But then came the rumour that would change everything; Dopey was missing. Alice rushed to see Nebby. She had to know what had happened.

'Nobody knows for sure,' Nebby told her. 'No one has seen him for a couple of days, but there are some grey feathers on the ground behind the house where he goes. Some say that Felix finally got his man.'

'Felix,' gasped Alice. 'I told Dopey not to taunt him.'

Alice flew to where feathers had been found, and sure enough, a solitary grey feather lay on the ground. She guessed that the rest had blown away in the wind. Alice took the feather in her claw.

'Dopey,' she sobbed. The feather was once her friend, but now he was just a feather. 'Dopey,' she sobbed again. 'I told you to be careful.' Alice gently placed the feather back on the ground, exactly as she had found it.

With her mind now in a blur, she flew up to the meeting tree. From there, she began a vigil in the hope that Dopey would return. It was hard to believe that he was now just a feather. She stared down at the feather, wishing it could talk.

It was late in the afternoon when the good Human came out of his house. He saw Alice sitting in the tree and threw some food onto the ground, but Alice was not feeling hungry. However, the food was not about to stay there long, because another Magpie then landed. This Magpie did not see Alice perched above, and he pounced on the food and scoffed it down.

'Welcome back, Broken Beak,' the good Human said, and then he threw some more food.

The Magpie hesitated. He did not trust the Human, but the offering was irresistible. He edged closer, all the time watching the Human. The Human glanced away, and in that instant, the Magpie grabbed the food and ran. From a safe distance, he scoffed his prize.

Alice was shocked, for she knew the Magpie that took the offering.

'Dad!' she squawked, 'you hypocrite. You told us never to take food from a Human, and yet that is what I find you doing.'

Albert looked up. He had been sprung. He thought this might happen one day, and he had long rehearsed what he would say. He played the sympathy card.

'You have to understand, Alice. It is tough for me. My beak makes hunting difficult, and for some time now, I have had to gather extra food for you lot.'

But Alice was in no mood to give her dad sympathy. She was in mourning for her friend, and her dad had treated that friend with scorn.

'You are pathetic,' she screamed. 'Look at you, frightened of a Human.'

Max was a short distance away, and he came to see why his sister was screaming. He arrived just in time to see Alice fly down from the tree. She walked up to the good Human and took food from his hand. Then she turned to her father. 'Dopey called me a scaredy-cat. I don't know what he would have called you. You are the most pathetic person I have ever met. You are nothing but a bully.'

This damning of the grand master might have been allowed to pass, had Max not been there to witness it. Albert had no choice. He had to exert his authority over this foolish girl. He rushed at Alice, and it was too late for her to escape, for he pounced the moment she paused to take off. With her attacker clinging to her back, Alice looked for a place of safety.

The Human's yard was divided into two levels, separated by a stone retaining wall. Concrete steps joined the levels, and the two Magpies rolled down those steps. Alice jammed her head into a corner where the bottom step butted against the wall, for she had to protect her eyes. She braced herself, claws spread firmly on the ground. Albert stayed clinging to her, and with forceful blows, he pecked at the back of her head.

Max did not know what to do, for he was too frightened to intervene. The Human watched on. He had often observed friendly jousts between Magpies, and they had always resolved themselves. It was not his place to interfere with natural behaviour. However, this attack seemed different. It was more violent. Suddenly, he had to act, for he could see feathers being torn out, and then he saw blood. 'Get off, shoo,' he yelled, and he kicked Albert with his foot.

Albert squawked and released Alice. He flapped his wings and leapt into the air, landing a short distance away. There he stood, glaring at Alice, but the Human ignored him.

The Human was crouched over Alice, not knowing if he should touch her. 'Are you alright,' he said, his voice soft and caring. Alice understood his concern, and she stood up. She was shaken and her head hurt, but she was still alive, and she still had eyes with which to see.

Albert looked at Max. 'We're out of here,' he said, and then he turned to Alice. 'You are banished from my kingdom. If I see you again; I will finish what I have started.' Then he looked back to Max. 'Come on, let's go.'

Max was faced with the hardest decision he would ever have to make. He looked at Alice, her eyes pleading for support, and then Albert stood between them. It was now his father's eyes that were glaring at him, and they were terrifying. He succumbed to the will of the grand master, and they left together.

As they flew away, Max consoled himself with the thought that Alice would be forgiven, but this he doubted. His brain began to numb. At that moment, the person he hated most in the world, was himself.

Alice watched him leave.

With no other place to go, Alice decided to stay in the meeting tree. She would have to live there and squawk if her father appeared. Hopefully, the good Human would come out and protect her. The Human's yard had a birdbath and a lawn. The lawn had tasty bugs, and the Human was generous with his food offerings. But Alice's life would be tied to that one place, a sad outlook for a girl who yearned to see the world.

20

ALICE LEAVES

The day that followed was a very different day for Max. He moped around, not knowing what to do. He missed his sister and could not face his friends, for they would ask about Alice, and he would have to tell them how he had abandoned her. He wondered if people already knew and were saying what a bad brother he was.

Meanwhile, Albert's mood remained unchanged. He was still angry. Muriel was not talking to him because of what he had done, but he was blaming Alice for all that had happened. Alice had challenged his authority and blown the free food deal that he had with the Human. He had unfinished business to settle with her.

Unfortunately, for Alice, the good Human was called away from his home that day. Alice's unlucky streak was continuing. With her guardian gone, she decided that she might as well risk a quick hunting trip down by the creek. Unlike her brother, she was a risk taker, and the creek was a place her father seldom visited. He mostly foraged in Gum Tree Park.

Albert was dining in the park when a Noisy Miner brought him a message. *Alice has not left the kingdom. She has made the good Human's yard her home, but is currently down by the creek, alone.* The Miners were always looking for ways to cause trouble among the Magpies.

Albert was furious. 'The time has come to finish what I started,' he squawked.

Max heard his father's decree and went into panic mode. 'Don't go to the creek,' he pleaded.

But Albert ignored his pleading son. 'Today, everyone will learn that the grand master cannot be disrespected.'

Max had to think quickly. He needed to buy Alice time and so he said, 'Dad, Mum often goes to the creek, and she might interfere if you attack Alice there. Why don't you go to the Human's yard and wait for her to return?'

'Good thinking,' said Albert. 'I might make a leader out of you yet.'

Albert flew off, leaving Max to wrestle with his conscience. Why had he not stepped in to protect Alice the first time their dad had attacked her? The two of them could have fought him off. What sort of a brother was he? Alice was right. He was afraid to take risks. Alice was brave, Dopey was brave; but he was just a scaredy-cat.

People think of growing up as a gradual process. Each day, you get a little bigger, a little stronger, a little smarter, but that was not how it happened for Max. He was afraid of his father, but he loved his sister more. He was not prepared to go through life without his sister, knowing that he could have saved her. That day, Max, the boy, watched his father leave to do unthinkable things to Alice, and moments later, a far more grown-up Max set out to be her protector.

Max found Alice scratching for worms by the side of the creek. He glided in, keeping close to the ground. She noted his low approach, for she had a nervous eye fixed on all that was happening about her. Seeing her brother brought joy to her heart, but he did not deserve a pleasant welcome. 'Very stealthy flying,' she said. 'Afraid someone might see you; someone like Dad, perhaps?'

'Yes,' said Max, 'but I don't care if he sees me, I just don't want him finding you.'

'Is he looking for me?'

'Thanks to the Miners, he already knows you are here and is waiting for you back by the meeting tree. You can't go back there. You have to get away.'

'But if I don't go back, he will know that you have warned me,' Alice reasoned.

'Don't care, just fly away.'

'Come with me,' Alice pleaded.

'I can't. I need to stay and tell Dad which direction you headed.'

'Why?'

'Because I will tell him the wrong way. That will buy you time.'

'But you will be in trouble when he works out what you have done.'

'Don't care,' Max said for a second time, and then he paused. 'Where will you go?'

Alice knew the answer to that. 'I will find the Great Gandor, and he will tell me how to get to the Great River.'

Max looked over his shoulder. Their dad would soon smell a rat and come looking. 'You must go, Sis, go.'

Alice felt the urgency. 'Bye, Maxie, wish me luck.'

She launched herself into the air, leaving along the same low trajectory her brother had used for his arrival. Max watched her turn towards the hills, and then he remembered that the Great Gandor ate people. He felt the urge to call her back, but a yell would attract their father.

He watched his sister until she was just a dot, merged against the patchwork of the hills, and then she was gone. She had left without his warning. 'Bye, Sis, good luck,' he whispered to himself, and then he flew to the meeting tree to tell his dad that he had just seen Alice heading for the city.

21

RETURNED FROM THE DEAD

A man called Murphy once discovered a law they called "Murphy's Law". This law warns that we should always allow for the unexpected, but Alice knew nothing of this law, and the unexpected happened the very next day.

Max went to the meeting tree where he discovered the good Human kneeling beside a box. Dopey was also next to the box, scoffing food from the Human's hand as if all was well in the world. Max flew down and glared at him.

'Where have you been? You are supposed to be dead. We had a memorial service and everything.'

Dopey was startled by the rude interruption. He was feeling fragile, and he never liked to be disturbed while eating. However, talk of his memorial service stopped him mid mouthful.

'You had a memorial service for me,' he stammered, 'and I was not there. I should have been there. How could you get the eulogy right without me? Was the eulogy good? Did many people go?'

'Just Nebby and me,' said Max, 'and we didn't bother about a eulogy.'

Dopey felt deflated. 'No crowd, no eulogy, how quick your friends forget. I don't suppose you want to know where I have been then, do you?'

'Tell me,' said Max, feeling annoyed that Dopey's absence had been the reason for all the bad things that had happened.

Dopey took a deep breath. 'Treachery,' he growled. 'I fell victim to the foulest treachery. I was playing tease the cat with Felix, and the rules state that the game is over once I walk away and begin pecking at the ground. Felix broke the rules.'

'What did he do?' asked Max, who was not surprised to hear that Felix had broken the rules, because Dopey was the only one who knew that any rules existed. Dopey took a second deep breath and continued.

'I had walked away from Felix and was standing close to the top of the retaining wall over there, and I did not notice Felix creep around behind me. He was crouching at the bottom of the wall, and when I peeped over the edge, he sprung, and I was done for. We had a terrible fight, and I lost a lot of feathers.'

'We noticed the feathers,' Max interrupted. 'We would have saved them had we known you were coming back.'

Dopey ignored Max's apology and went on to explain how the good Human had rushed to his rescue. He remembered seeing feathers fly, and when he realised that the feathers were his, he fainted. Next, he woke up in a box, and when the box was opened, he found himself in a strange place where birds and animals were being kept in cages. He was put in a cage beside them.

Dopey then told how two aliens were doing strange experiments on their captives. The aliens were Human in shape but wore white suits and their faces were covered.

Max had his doubts. Everyone knew that Dopey was obsessed with aliens. A wise old Owl who gained much of his wisdom by watching movies at the local drive in, had informed Dopey of their existence.

'They could have been Humans,' Max suggested.

'No,' said Dopey. 'I could tell they were aliens because their suits did not cover their hands. Their hands were made of rubber.'

Max was not convinced, but Dopey was never going to change his story. He pushed on with his questions, for that is what a good detective does. 'How did you get away?' he asked.

'I don't know,' said Dopey. 'All I know is that they eventually put me back in this box.'

'What then?'

'Don't know,' Dopey said again. 'Next time the box opened, I jumped out and here I am.' Dopey glared at the box. 'Whatever you do, don't get in that box, it is an alien shuttlecraft.'

Max noted Dopey's concern and stepped away from the object under suspicion. 'I will avoid the box,' he said.

However, the detective in Max still had doubts, for nothing Dopey said ever made sense. Unfortunately, neither knew that good Humans sometimes treat Mother Nature's creatures in their veterinary hospitals.

Max decided to give Dopey a sharp taste of reality and told how Alice had been banished.

Dopey looked sad. 'That's too bad,' he said. 'I would have liked to have told her something before she went.'

'Too late,' said Max. 'You have lost your chance.'

Max had no sympathy for Dopey. Alice would still be there had she not lost her temper with her dad, but thinking that Dopey was dead had made her reckless. Dopey was irresponsible, and his irresponsibility had cost Alice dearly.

The Human picked up the box and went back into his house, leaving Dopey and Max to face each other. 'Alice stayed here all day thinking you were dead,' Max squawked.

'Oh no,' said Dopey. 'I told her never to come here in the afternoons, because that is when her dad comes here. I knew bad things would happen if she ever discovered the truth about him.'

Max spread his wings in anger. 'Well, bad things did happen because she thought you were dead. Everything is your fault. I hope your stupidity has taught you something.'

Dopey looked towards the place that had been the scene of his almost demise. 'Sure has,' he said. 'I will stay away from the top of that wall in future.' With that, he stretched his wings to see that they still worked, and then he flew away.

'I don't think that bird will ever grow up,' Max mumbled to himself.

22

THE REBEL

In the months that followed, Max often thought about Alice, and he would look towards the hills. She was somewhere over that distant ridge, looking for the Great Gandor. Sometimes, he would tell himself that she was seeing the world, doing the thing she most wanted. At other times, he felt sad. He wondered if she was safe or whether the Great Gandor had eaten her. But mostly, he just missed her.

It was while sitting in the meeting tree, the place where Max always went to think about Alice, that he noticed something strange. Dead leaves and sticks were spraying out from under a bush, making an untidy mess on the ground. Max had seen such messes before. He believed them to be the work of a secretive group of birds, an underground resistance movement that was doing what it could to upset the Humans, for the mess seemed to annoy them. The Humans were always sweeping the mess away, but the rebels made it their business to see that it was soon back again.

These suspicions had brought out the detective in Max, and he had always wanted to track down the culprits. Now was his chance. He flew down and peeped beneath the bush. Almost at once, a small stone whizzed past his head, followed by some leaves and a twig. Max retreated beyond the range of the flying debris and took a second peek. Through a spray of dirt and leaves, he saw the bouncing backside of a bird, its owner franticly scratching the ground.

'What are you doing?' Max asked.

The bird spun around and crouched low, peering at Max from under the bush.

'Good day,' said the bird. 'I'm just scratching up a feed. My name is B2. My folks called us B1, B2, and B3, because we are Blackbirds. Last year, my folks called their kids Blackie One, Blackie Two, and Blackie Three. This year, they got lazy.'

Max had never met a Blackbird before. *Talkative fellow*, he thought. *I think I just got his life story.* He introduced himself. 'My name is Max, and I am a Magpie.'

'Mum loves Magpies,' said B2.

Max was flattered. 'My mum likes Kookaburras,' he said. 'What do you think your mum will call her kids next year?'

'Mum is not having any more kids,' B2 laughed. 'She says she is sick of the mess we make. Sometimes, Mum says she'd love to have a Magpie as a kid, but they tell her she can only have Blackbirds. Mum says that Mother Nature's rules are very annoying.'

B2 stayed crouched beneath the bush and continued talking about his mum. 'Mum would like you,' he said. 'Perhaps I could take you home for Mum to adopt.'

The sad reality of Max's home life flashed through his mind. *Too late now*, he thought. *I am all grown up and Alice has been kicked out of home.*

'Given my dad's attitude to life, that is an offer I should think about,' Max said in jest. 'How about you come out from under the bush, and we have a chat.'

'Still hungry,' said B2. 'You keep talking, and I'll keep scratching.'

Max discovered that he had many things in common with this rebel. They both thought worms were good to eat, they both liked to sing, and they both disliked the Miners. B2 said that the Miners did not bother him much because Blackbirds foraged under bushes and stayed out of the Miner's way.

Max found B2 to be a likable chap, except for the way that he threw things at his visitors. However, bad manners seemed to be something they had in common. Max never made a good first impression, and B2 was unaware that showering people with rubbish was unsociable behaviour.

Max wondered if B2 and he could become good friends, but then a small gum nut hit him in the head. It was time to leave. He farewelled B2, saying that he would catch up sometime when B2 was not eating.

He returned to Gum Tree Park, the place that was his home, and he looked towards his old nest tree, the student dormitory, and the seat where Brian had face planted. *How did our happy family fall apart?* he wondered, and then he looked towards his father's throne.

23

HARD TIMES

Time passed slowly for Max after Alice left. She had gone in the Living Time when the days were longer. Max wondered if the days were really longer, or if boredom simply made them seem longer, for nothing was the same without his sister. He tried having fun with his friends, but no one could replace Alice.

Charlie was no fun because a bird stuck in a cage could not go anywhere. B2 seemed fun but was always throwing stuff at people. Willy liked fun but was never still long enough to have a conversation, and Murray was scary. There were plenty of Miners about, but they only wanted a fight. Dopey was the closest person Max knew to a normal bird, and Max wondered why it was that only Magpies were normal.

At one point, Gum Tree Park experienced an influx of new birds. They came in large flocks to feast on the flowers that suddenly appeared on the gum trees. Max introduced himself to Honey Eaters, Budgerigars, and Parrots, but they were all too busy eating to talk to him. They destroyed the flowers in no time, and then they left.

Then came the Dying Time and hunting became harder. The bugs, grasshoppers, and crawlies, mostly disappeared. Food became scarce, but there were still the subterranean creatures. The softer ground made them easier to dig out, and Max was now a good hunter. The days also became colder, and shorter. In one way, the shorter days were good, for it meant Max spent more time sleeping, saving the precious energy he needed to fight out the cold.

The Dying Time saw the Humans mostly sheltering in their houses. Some nights, the air would freeze, the rain would pour, and the wind would howl, but the Humans were untouched by all this. They were warm and asleep in their beds, and they seldom gave thought to the birds, or wondered how hardy birds had to be. The birds would be outside, huddled together, their feathers fluffed to keep out the cold. They would cling to branches, be buffeted by the wind, and they would feel the chill of the freezing rain as it drove through their trees. But come morning, the Humans would wake and hear the birds rejoicing in the first rays of the morning sun.

However, not everything died in the Dying Time, for that was when the creek came to life. Its water flowed once more, and tall grass appeared on its banks. Max was fascinated by the creek. He would watch the water flow by, wondering where the water had come from and where it was going, and he would listen to the tall grass as it rustled in the winter breeze. Unfortunately, this was all that Max could find to enjoy. Winter had come as a shock to him, for the whole world seemed to be dying. However, Grandma was quick to set him straight. 'Don't worry, Max, nothing stays the same forever,' she would say.

Grandma was old and had seen the seasons come and go many times. She told Max that he needed to stay strong and not worry about the future. Today was all that mattered.

Then the Living Time began again. Grandma was right; nothing stays the same. Max felt a new warmth coming from the sun, and tiny shoots began to appear on the trees. The air was filled with a strange magic. The world of Max's early childhood was coming back, and it made him feel good. His fun-loving spirit was returning.

24

MAYZIE

It was while under the spell of spring that Max met a kindred spirit. Her name was Mayzie, a young lady Magpie who had been raised in a nearby kingdom. Like Alice, she was keen to leave home and see the world. However, she had gotten no further than the meeting tree before having thoughts about settling down. The meeting tree had potential, and it came with a pre-installed male, namely, Max. But it took some time for Mayzie to catch Max's attention, for he pretended not to notice her.

Max felt sad whenever Mayzie perched in the meeting tree, for it had been Alice's tree. Her banishment meant that she could no longer go there, but this out-of-town Magpie could come and go as she pleased. It all seemed so unfair.

Eventually, it occurred to Max that Mayzie always appeared whenever he went to the tree. Was this a coincidence, or was she looking out for him? Max wondered if he should feel flattered. Perhaps he had an admirer.

Normally, the gentleman makes the first move, but Mayzie could see that Max was a slow mover, and she was a bird who did not like to beat around the bush. Having given him more come-ons than she thought necessary, she finally resorted to the direct approach and perched alongside him.

'Hello, Max, my name is Mayzie. Do you come here often?'

Max thought this to be an odd question because he knew that Mayzie had seen him there many times. However, his ego caused him to excuse the ridiculous nature of her question. *She knows my name*, he thought. *I do have an admirer.*

'Yep, I come here a bit,' he said, trying to sound cool.

'Hoping to find someone special?' Mayzie asked, flickering her eyes as she spoke.

Suddenly, all sad thoughts of Alice vanished. Max's heart jumped, but unfortunately, his reply was not what Mr Cool would have said.

'I'm hoping to find Alice.'

Max knew nothing about pick-up-lines and a possible romance almost ended there and then, but Mayzie was a tenacious bird. She decided to give the idiot one last chance for redemption.

Max told her the story about Alice, successfully climbing out of the hole he had dug for himself. Mayzie sympathised, and she was moved by Max's dedication to his sister. After a brief show of empathy, she pushed the conversation along.

'You know,' she said, 'I have had my eye on this tree for some time. There is an excellent fork in that branch. It would make an ideal place for me to build a nest.'

Max had no idea what Mayzie was talking about. *Why would anyone want to build a nest?* he thought. *I gave up living in a nest long ago.* He gave Mayzie a puzzled look. 'That would be a waste of time,' he said.

Mayzie had discovered all that she needed to know about Mr Cool. He was too young, but she was patient. She could see that the boy had potential; he just had to grow up a little. *Maybe next year*, she thought. *Meanwhile, I will make sure that no other bird gets her claws into him.*

25

BANISHMENT

Max was living in the moment, and it was a good moment. Grandma had told him not to worry about the future, and she was right. Spring was a good moment to be living in, and he would have been happy for it to last forever. However, an unfortunate comment made by Grandma was overheard by Albert, and it caused Max's world to come crashing around him.

Grandma had spicy gossip to tell Muriel. 'I saw young Maxie yesterday,' she said with a tone of mischief. 'I know where he sneaks off to every day.'

Muriel was interested.

'He has a young lady,' said Grandma. 'I think they make a fine couple. Max could be our next grand master.'

It was those last few words that sealed Max's fate. Albert knew what he had to do. He was not getting any younger, and a day would come when a younger bird would successfully challenge to be grand master. In the past, he had managed to identify such rivals and drive them out before they were strong enough to challenge. Max was marked for banishment.

Max arrived home that evening without a worry in the world. That was, until Albert pounced. Max was attacked with the same ferocity that had be-felled his sister. A savage fight followed, and Albert discovered that Max was already the stronger bird. However, Max did not have the fighting guile of his father, nor did he have a willingness to hurt his opponent. He respected his dad.

'You are banished, you are banished, be gone from this place forever,' Albert shouted, his judgement echoing through the trees.

Max ran to the edge of the park, and there he stopped and looked back to his mother, but her eyes were pleading for him to leave. 'You have to go,' she said. 'Go find your sister. Make sure that she is safe.'

'But I don't want to leave,' Max spluttered.

'You have to. It is the Magpie way. Just remember all that we have taught you.'

'I will, Mum, but I don't want to leave you here.'

Muriel understood. 'I will miss you too, but you must go. I can take care of myself.'

Albert rushed at Max again.

'Go,' Muriel yelled, and then she repeated her plea once more. 'Go find Alice,' she cried.

Max took to the air, thinking those would be the last words he would ever hear his mother say, for his father's voice was now the only voice he could hear. Albert was warbling his song of victory.

Max left, unsure of what had just happened, but he wished that there had been time to give his mother a better goodbye.

26

FAREWELL TO FRIENDS

Max needed someone to put him up for the night, and he decided to try Nebby. He found him clinging to a thin branch, high above the ground. It was the first time that he had seen Nebby on the move.

Max chose a more solid branch on which to perch, for Nebby's branch looked like it could snap at any moment.

'That looks a bit risky,' Max warned.

Nebby ignored the warning, for he was too busy chewing. After several more chews, he swallowed and then replied, 'A feller has to eat, and these new leaves near the top are the best.'

'You eat leaves?' Max queried. 'That certainly explains the eucalyptus breath.'

Nebby frowned. He was sick of hearing comments about his breath. The Crows were always poking fun at him and asking if sucking lozenges helped his sore throat. Nebby never understood the joke because he never had a sore throat, nor did he suck lozenges. He regarded Crows as having a weird sense of humour and thought that they were merely jealous of his excellent lifestyle.

'I live in a restaurant, which is very convenient,' Nebby explained. 'I never have to leave home, which means I can spend all day thinking.'

More like sleeping, thought Max, but he kept the thought to himself. 'What about drinking?' he asked.

Nebby paused his next mouthful. 'I only go out for a drink when I get thirsty, but most days, I get enough juice from the leaves.'

'But what if you fall?'

Max's questions were becoming annoying. Apparently, he was unaware that it was rude to interrupt someone while they were eating. A polite person would wait until Nebby had finished his meal, sometime closer to dawn. 'Bears bounce,' Nebby snapped, hoping an abrupt reply might end the conversation, but subtlety always went over Max's head.

'But you are not a bear, you are a Koala.'

I am not getting into that discussion, thought Nebby. He frowned at Max. 'Look, if you want a place to roost for the night, be my guest, but don't interrupt me while I am eating.'

Max took the hint and found a branch that looked comfortable. He settled for the night, but sleep eluded him. It was hard to relax with Nebby crashing about the place. Not satisfied with one branch, Nebby had checked them all by morning, looking for succulent leaves. At one point the wind sprung up, and Max heard a faint yippee. He peeped through a squinted eye and saw Nebby on the very end of the highest branch, swaying back and forth in the wind.

You never really know a person until you live with them, thought Max. *I thought Nebby was wise, but he is actually a bit of a fruitcake.*

Max thought about moving to another tree, but he did not want to risk stumbling into a clan of sleeping Miners. He had had enough fighting for one day. Then he heard Willy in the distance and thought about going there, but Willy was in party mode and Max was in no mood for a party. He had no choice other than to stay as Nebby's guest. Next morning, he told Nebby of his banishment.

'Where will you go?' asked Nebby, shocked that Max had been thrown out of home.

Max looked towards the hills. 'I am going to find Alice.'

'You don't know where to look,' said Nebby.

Max disagreed. 'I will seek out the Great Gandor, for that is where she would have gone first.'

'Oh no!' Nebby exclaimed.

'What?' snapped Max.

'If she comes face to face with the Great Gandor, he will eat her.'

'She knows that risk,' said Max, 'but she wants to get to the Great River and only the Great Gandor knows the way.'

'Who told you that?' asked Nebby, looking puzzled.

'You did,' said Max.

Nebby dug into the recesses of his memory, trying to recall the relevant conversation.

'I did? Perhaps I did, but you must understand, that is all Crows' talk. Crows are the ones who talk about the Great Gandor and the Great River, but Crows often lie.'

Max had to look away, for he felt a surge of anger towards his friend. However, this would be the last time that he would see Nebby, and he did not want to leave on a sour note.

'True or not, that is what Alice believes, and that is what she will do,' Max replied.

Nebby had taken a doubtful story told by the Crows and repeated it as fact. He had done it to appear wise, not knowing that it would have unforeseen consequences. If the Crows were telling the truth, Alice and Max would be eaten, and if they were lying, they would be lost forever. Alice could have resettled closer to home, but Nebby had caused her to go looking for something that might not exist, and Max was about to make the same mistake.

'You must run if the Great Gandor tries to eat you,' Nebby warned.

'That will only be a problem if the Great Gandor actually exists,' laughed Max, trying to disguise how upset he was.

Nebby hung his head, for he did not know what to say.

Max had known Nebby for most of his life, yet he did not really know him at all. Nebby could sit motionless for hours, thinking about all things scientific. At other times, he could be a branch swinging rodeo star. Some called him a Koala, some called him a bear, but at that particular moment, Max saw him as a sad little creature that was full of self-doubt. He thanked Nebby for trying to teach him manners and then left, for he had several more stops to make, and his father would soon come looking for him.

Max went to the meeting tree where he knew he would find Mayzie. As always, she was waiting for him. He told her how his father had attacked him for no apparent reason, and how he had been banished. He said that he was off to find his sister and asked if she wanted to come with him.

Mayzie listened, and then came up with her much better idea. She suggested that they make a home in the meeting tree because it stood just outside Albert's kingdom, but Max was too young to be a family man. He still wanted to be an adventurer, and he wanted to find his sister.

Mayzie had a decision to make. Does she go with the dashing young man whose qualities include kindness, empathy, and loyalty, or does she stay with her tree. She chose her tree. Max turned, and in the style befitting an epic romance, he flew out of her life.

Charlie was next on Max's list, but Max decided to give Charlie a miss. Mayzie's preference for a tree had left him deflated, and the last thing he wanted was for someone to tell him that the world was an unfriendly place. This left only Dopey.

Max found Dopey on Slingshot Sam's antenna, doing his morning target practice. He greeted Max in his usual, casual manner.

'Have a shot,' he said. The target got a bit washed away in the recent rain. Any assistance to rebuild would be greatly appreciated.'

Max obliged, and then told Dopey how his father had banished him, and that he was now off to find Alice. Dopey felt tempted to join Max in his quest, but Doves were not renowned adventurers. He had already survived an alien abduction, but no one believed him. *What is the point in having an adventure if no one believes the tale?* he thought.

Dopey wished Max good luck, but just as Max was about to leave, he had an afterthought.

'Wait,' he said.

'What?' said Max.

'Tell Alice when you find her, that Dopey said she is not a scaredy-cat.' Dopey sounded soulful, not at all Dopey-like.

'Okay,' said Max, as he took off. Once airborne, he looked back. Dopey was waving goodbye.

Max wondered about the strange message, but Dopey was a strange bird. The hills stood before him, and beyond was the unknown.

Alice was somewhere in that unknown, and he was going to find her. He was about to become a great, Magpie adventurer.

27

A DIFFERENT WORLD

Max decided to follow the creek that came down from the hills, for it offered trees for shelter, places to hunt, and more water than he could ever drink. His journey would be a series of short flights, taking care not to fly too high, for there was always a risk of being attacked by a bird of prey. Between each flight, he would rest and forage for food.

By the evening of the first day, he had reached the foot of the hills. He slept that night, the first that he had ever slept alone. He was tired but was comforted in the knowledge that there were other Magpies about. He had no idea whose kingdom he was in, but he had told all those he had met along the way, that he was just a simple traveller passing through. He asked if anyone had seen Alice, but none had. He guessed that his search would not be easy.

Next morning, he was woken by a familiar ceremony, the Welcome of the Dawn. *Dad was right*, he thought, *Magpies do it everywhere*. It made him feel homesick. *Why did dad banish me?* he wondered.

Then Max noticed something unusual. He could see the gums of his old home in the distance, bathed by the first rays of the sun. However, the sun's rays had yet to reach where he was, and he thought this unfair. The sun rose from behind the hills, and he was now closer to the hills than those living at Gum Tree Park, yet they were seeing the sun rise first. Max wished that Nebby was there to explain the scientific reason for the sun's lack of fairness.

Once the ceremony was over, Max had a quick breakfast of beetles and then continued to follow the creek. He guessed that was what Alice would have done. Alice wanted to find the Great River, and she may have reasoned that the creek would lead her to something bigger. However, he wondered if the creek went much further, for when he looked ahead, he could not see it. Logic told him that it would be on the hill's face, for it had nowhere else to be, but it was not there.

Detective Max flew on, but unlike the mystery of his delayed sun rise, this case he solved. The creek had found a gap in the hills, and the gap was the entrance to a gorge. Max flew into the gorge and therein found a world far different to that of rooftops and fences. The creeks previously placid water was now gushing and gurgling between rocks and reeds. In some places, it meandered, in others, it spilled over large boulders. In one place, it fell in a cascade of sparkling white, sounding like nothing Max had ever heard; a loud sound, and yet somehow, it was peaceful.

The creek had led him to a place beyond everything he had ever known, and he wondered why he had ever doubted his sister. She was right in her yearning to see the world. He marvelled at his surroundings. The hills were no longer in front, but on either side, and in some places, they were sheer. The gorge was bursting with life, full of bushes and trees, and the air was fresh, smelling of earth, leaves, and flowers. Max flew above the trees to see what lay ahead, but he could see no further than the next bend.

Then Max was touched by a moment of sadness. He was sharing his experience with no one, and he wished that Mayzie had come with him. He wondered if he would ever see his old friends again, and he briefly fantasised how he might one day describe the gorge to them. Then he thought about Alice and wondered if she had seen this place. After that, he decided to stop thinking, for his thoughts were telling him an uncomfortable truth—he was now all alone in the world.

Max followed the creek until it was no longer in the gorge. Instead, it meandered through a broad valley set between rolling hills. Then, close to dark, he came upon a bridge; the first evidence of Humans he had seen all day. This out of place structure was a sad reminder on how Humans spoil Mother Nature's beauty, a disappointing finale to having just experienced one of her wonderful creations.

Max chose a tree to camp for the night, for he had a decision to make. The creek was now a mere trickle, and in some places, it disappeared altogether in the long grass. He could see that it would soon end, and he would need something else to follow.

A narrow road ran across the bridge, and the road seemed a logical choice, but in which direction was the problem. *What would Alice have done?* He did not know the answer, but he hoped that it would come to him in the morning.

28

NEVER TRUST A CROW

Max woke the next day to the sound of distant carolling. The morning ceremony that had annoyed him as a child, was now music to his ears. *Magpies have settled everywhere*, he thought. *No wonder we have the Noisy Miners bluffed.* But he still had a problem, for he did not know which way to go. He would have to trust his instincts and let Mother Nature be his guide.

That morning, Mother Nature had caused a gentle breeze to blow along the road, and he felt she might be offering it to help him on his way. He accepted the offer, but then wondered where the road would take him.

Eventually, the road joined up to a highway. There, Max found cars, trucks, and buses, all travelling at great speeds in both directions, but he needed to know which were coming from the city, for the city was not a place where he would find the Great Gandor. Then he caught a whiff of the city on the breeze. Mother Nature was helping him again, for he now knew which way led from the city.

Max followed the highway, stopping at times to rest his wings and forage for food. He knew all the best eating-places back home, but the eateries along the highway were poor. He pushed on, hoping to find a good restaurant.

Then he came across something unusual. Three Crows were huddled on the bitumen, and Max had an eerie feeling about them, for he felt that Crows had been watching him all day. They seemed to know he was coming, and he wondered if news of his progress was being passed along.

One of the huddled Crows looked up and waved a wing, beckoning Max to join them. Max landed a short distance from the group.

'What are you doing in this part of the world, son?' asked the Crow doing the beckoning. The greeting was neither friendly nor unfriendly, but it made Max nervous.

'I am looking for a nice eatery, any suggestions?'

The Crows all laughed and then the talkative Crow spoke once more. 'The best we can offer around here are the pop-up food stands.' The talkative Crow returned to the huddle and Max heard a snigger.

'Where do you suggest I look?' Max asked, hoping to get their attention again.

The talkative Crow turned. 'This is the only food stand open today, son, and you had better hurry. They are almost out of food.'

The Crows laughed some more.

'Why would they put a food stand in the middle of a highway?' Max asked.

There was another burst of laughter, and then the talkative Crow spoke again.

'Son, new food stands pop up along the highway every day, but they never stay in business long. They belong to a franchise we call the Roadkill Cafes. Unfortunately, not many have been opening lately. I think they are going through a recession, but if things go right, this one should be getting a fresh delivery shortly.'

There was more Crows' laughter.

Max felt uneasy, and he stood there, puzzled. He was among friends, but they were not his, and he did not understand why they were laughing. Nebby had experienced the same problem with Crows and their throat lozenge joke. Crows had a weird sense of humour. Max wondered if there really was a Roadkill Cafes franchise, or if the Crows were making it up. He decided to change the subject.

'Have any of you seen a Magpie called Alice pass this way?' he asked.

The laughter stopped. Max heard a mumble coming from within the huddle and then the two non-speaking Crows suddenly spoke in turn.

'Yes, she went that way.'

'No, she went the other way.'

'That was when she was flying in a circle.'

'No, that was when she was flying backwards.'

'Quiet,' shouted the talkative Crow, who Max had determined to be the leader. The talkative Crow looked at Max again. 'I am sorry, my boys are easily confused, but we have not seen an Alice person pass this way. Is there something else we can help you with?'

Charlie's warning echoed in Max's head. *It is an unfriendly world out there.*

'Do you know where I can find the Great Gandor?' Max asked.

'The Great who?' came the response.

'The Great Gandor. He sees all. He is a legend in this part of the world.'

'Never heard of him,' said the talkative Crow. He turned to his boys. 'Either of you boys heard of the Great Gandor?'

'Nup.'

'Nope.'

This time they agreed.

The talkative Crow shrugged. 'Sorry, son, we cannot help you with that, but perhaps you would join us for a meal.'

The huddle opened and Max could see a lump of red flesh packed in grey fur. The Crows had been pecking at it.

The talkative Crow continued. 'This unfortunate creature met his demise here this morning, and we have been tasked with the job of removing his mortal remains before his poor mother comes upon them.'

The Crows resumed their laughter.

At last, Max thought he understood Crow humour. The pop-up food stands were the bodies of dead animals, but the things that amused Crows showed flaws in their character. They cared not for the feelings of a mother. Max, who knew nothing about tact, expressed his opinion on their joke.

'How can you care about the feelings of a mother when you are eating her child?'

The two boys looked to their wiser father, knowing he would have the answer, and he did.

'Son, it is an ethical problem that has troubled many, but Crows have two words to cover it—natural recycling. We are natural recyclers, and what we are doing here is recycling. If we do not recycle, the world will one day run out of food.'

Max saw some logic in the argument, but he wondered if that was because he was hungry. He stared at the unfortunate creature, and then he heard the sound of a large truck coming towards them.

'Stay here and think about it, son. Roadkill is fantastic food. We are off for a drink but will be back shortly. Oh, and don't worry about the truck, it will go around you, they always do.'

The Crows departed, leaving Max to look at the meal they had left. The truck drew closer. Suddenly, Max heard a voice coming from a bush beside the road.

'Get out of there or you will be run over.'

It was a sweet voice, a tweet. It was not a voice of authority. Such a voice could never tell a Magpie what to do. Max ignored it, and the roar of the truck became louder. Then he heard the voice again.

'Max, follow me.'

The tiniest bird Max had ever seen was standing beside him. His head was a brilliant blue, and his upright tail reminded him of Willy. *How does he know my name?* Max thought. The bird flew away, and Max followed. Moments later, the truck flattened the furry bundle that could have been Max's meal.

29

TINKER AND TINKALINA

The little bird sat next to Max, looking towards the squashed remains.

'Those trucks will never go around you know. You were the Crows' next meal. They try that trick on every unsuspecting traveller.'

Max shuddered as he looked down at the little bird who had just saved his life, a hero in miniature who had put himself in the path of danger. 'How do you know my name?' he asked.

'We guessed you were Max when we heard you asking the Crows about Alice. Alice told us all about you.' The little bird then began hopping in a circle, as if standing still was not an option. He introduced himself. 'My name is Tinker.'

Max was stunned, for he could hardly believe what was happening. Moments before, a truck had almost killed him, and now this little bird was telling him the most amazing news. Mother Nature had led him to someone who knew Alice, and that someone had said, 'Us'. This meant that Tinker knew others who also knew Alice.

'Who is us?' Max asked, his voice almost quivering.

'You must come and meet my wife, and we will tell you about Alice.'

Max's heart skipped a beat, for Tinker's excitement was infectious. He was daring to think that Alice might be nearby.

Tinker hopped over to a bush and with the sweetest tweet he could muster, he tweeted, 'Tinkalina, Tinkalina.'

Max waited in anticipation, for Tinker was the most elegant little bird he had ever met, and he wondered if someone called Tinkalina might be even more elegant. The birds that raided Gum Tree Park for its flowers had more colours, but Tinker's dainty form and striking blue markings made him special.

Tinkalina hopped out of the bush. She was elegant and tiny, just like her husband, but her plumage was common brown and grey. Max was disappointed. He bowed graciously towards her.

'Very pleased to meet you,' he said. 'What happened to your pretty feathers?'

Max had learnt nothing from his first meeting with Mayzie, for he was clueless when it came to talking to the opposite sex. He was trying to improve his manners, but his lack of tact often got him into trouble.

Tinkalina frowned. 'Men, you are all the same. You don't realise that Mother Nature makes you the pretty ones because you have nothing else going for you.'

Tinker, who had been hopping in circles, headed for a bush. His wife gave a sharp tweet and he stopped, turned, and slowly hopped back.

'Sorry,' said Max. 'You are very pretty. I just thought it a little unfair that Tinker was the one who got to wear the fancy dress.'

'Apology accepted,' said Tinkalina, and then she turned to her husband. 'It would be nice if you told me sometimes that I looked pretty.'

Tinker hopped behind Max. He needed to create a diversion for things were not going well for him. He waved a wing and gestured that everyone follow. 'Come on, we know a place with lots of grubs,' he said. 'I reckon a Magpie could snare a few of them with his long beak.'

Tinker darted off with Tinkalina in pursuit. Max followed. There was no way that he was letting them out of his sight, for they knew about Alice. They also knew the whereabouts of grubs, and Max was hungry.

The three birds landed in the middle of a clearing and Max went into hunting mode. He stood frozen, his senses on full alert. The next grub to move would meet a sudden death. The little birds hopped around him, each trying to out tweet the other, but Tinkalina was by far the more vocal.

'We are Blue-wrens,' she said. 'Tinker says that girls should not be called Blue-wrens because girls are not blue, but I just tell him to keep his opinions to himself.'

'Please be quiet while I hunt for grubs,' Max whispered, trying to ignore Tinkalina's chatter, but Tinkalina continued with no adjustment to her volume.

'I thought you wanted to know about Alice?'

'Let the man eat,' interrupted Tinker.

Max paused. Tinkalina was right. He was putting his personal hunger above his quest, which was not the way of a true adventurer. He relaxed his hunting stance and apologised. 'I can eat later,' he said. 'The grubs will be easier to catch when the sun cools a little. What can you tell me about Alice?'

Tinker began. 'Well—'

Tinkalina interrupted. 'It's like this—'

'Who is telling this story?' asked Tinker.

'I am,' said Tinkalina. 'Men always get their stories wrong.'

Tinker commenced hopping in a circle once more. 'Sorry dear,' he mumbled.

Tinkalina continued. 'Alice passed this way some time back. We met her in this very clearing, catching grubs.'

'Did she stay long?' Max asked.

'A few days,' said Tinkalina, 'for she was not sure where to go next. She was asking about the Great Gandor and the Great River.'

'She caught lots of grubs,' Tinker added.

'That is irrelevant to the story,' snapped Tinkalina.

Tinker continued to hop in a circle.

'So where did she go?' Max asked.

Tinkalina went on. 'She wanted to find the Great River.'

Tinker felt compelled to interrupt. 'That is not where she was going.'

Tinkalina glared at her husband. 'She had to find the Great Gandor first,' she added.

'That's right,' said Tinker.

Tinkalina frowned. 'I was just getting to that bit you silly man.'

Tinker continued to hop in a circle.

Max was excited for their stories confirmed that he was on the right track, but he worried what would happen once Alice found the Great Gandor.

'Can you tell me about the Great Gandor?' he asked.

'Oh yes,' said Tinker, pausing part way through a circle.

'He sees everything,' said Tinkalina.

'And he eats people,' added Tinker.

'Anything else?' asked Max.

'No, that's it,' said Tinker. 'That's all we know. Alice didn't tell us any more.'

'But he is a legend,' Max went on.

'Not around here,' said Tinkalina.

'We had never heard of him before Alice told us about him,' Tinker added.

This was an unexpected setback. The Crows said that they did not know about the Great Gandor, even though Crows were the ones who had first told Nebby the story. Now, the Blue-wrens were saying the same thing. How can the Great Gandor be a legend if no one had ever heard of him, and how could Max find someone that no one had ever heard of? He was left with just one question.

'How did Alice propose to find the Great Gandor?' he asked.

Tinkalina answered. 'She said that she would follow the highway until she found someone who knew his whereabouts.'

Max now had a plan. He would do the same as Alice. For the first time since leaving home, he knew for sure which way she had gone. He felt relieved, and he chatted with the Blue-wrens until roosting time. However, his sleep that night was almost non-existent, for he found something new to worry him.

The sun appeared to be in trouble, and Max knew that the world would end if anything bad ever happened to it. He had been taught that the sun always rises on one side of the world and disappears on the other. The only mystery was how it got back to start at the same place next morning. Most thought it used magic, but Nebby's explanation was more scientific. He said that it had a tunnel.

Max had fallen asleep soon after sunset, but he stirred when he sensed a glow of dawn. Magpies have to be awake to welcome the sun's return. He shook himself to alertness but then discovered that the sun was about to rise from the same place to where it had set. He continued watching, but the glow remained the same. Slowly, he reasoned that the sun had become stuck in the ground. He watched the glow all night. At times, he dozed, but each time he peeped out, the glow was still there. The sun was trapped, but then came the proper dawn, and the sun appeared in its usual place. Max was relieved. The sun was unharmed, and the world would see another day. He welcomed it as never before.

Max joined Tinker in the clearing and enjoyed a breakfast of grubs. During breakfast, he asked Tinker if he had seen the unusual glow in the sky.

'That is always there,' Tinker explained. 'It is the glow of the Civilized World, and it comes from the city. Some say that Humans are afraid of the dark and so they make their own light while the sun is resting. You can always work out the whereabouts of Humans by looking for their lights at night.'

Max was relieved to hear that the sun had not met with misfortune, and he now had a way of detecting Humans from afar. He asked Tinker if Tinkalina would be joining them.

Tinker sounded a little sad. 'Tinkalina is feeling a bit off colour this morning,' he explained, 'and she has asked me to say goodbye. She is not usually that grumpy you know, but her migraines have been giving her a bad time lately.'

Max left shortly after breakfast, and Tinker tweeted him farewell.

What a lovely couple, Max thought as he flew away. Tinker was the most understanding, henpecked husband Max had ever met. Who would have thought that such a tiny bird would turn out to be a superhero who wore a blue mask and saved travellers from the clutches of the evil Crows?

30

LOFTY THE LOST

Max set out along the highway. So far, Mother Nature had not let him down. He looked into the bushes as they passed beneath his wings, wondering where she might be hiding. He could feel her presence, keeping him on the right path. Then a beautiful sound came drifting through the air. *Is that you, Mother Nature?* he thought.

Max flew towards the sound and came upon a large building. It was white, with a sharply angled roof. There was a sign out the front, but Max could not read signs. He had no way of knowing that he was gazing upon the Church of Nowhere.

The Church of Nowhere was built in the middle of nowhere, a perfect example of Human logic. The Humans of the district could never agree on which of their settlements should host the district's church, and so they built it in the middle of nowhere, which pleased no one.

Max perched on the sign, for the beautiful sound was coming from inside the church. The front door was open, and he could see Humans, and they were singing. Max was amazed, for this was the first time that he had heard a group of Humans sing. He thought these had to be happy Humans, unlike the ones back home, who must have all been sad.

He gazed at the singers, but then he caught a movement out of the corner of his eye. A short distance away was a head attached to a long neck. It was tilted, its owner peering at him from behind a bush. The head was almost the size of a Magpie, and it had a beak. A monster bird was staring at him. Max felt a shudder of excitement, for it had to be the Great Gandor. Mother Nature had shown him the way.

Max flew to a high branch to survey his surroundings. The monster bird was standing in the church graveyard, and on one gravestone stood the statue of an angel. Max wondered at the angel's wings. *A flying Human*, he thought, but he had no time to dwell on such a mystery. The giant bird demanded his attention.

The bird had long legs and was as tall as a Human. His feathers were scrawny and dark, but his wings were tiny, too tiny to carry him in flight. He appeared to be trapped in the yard, because the yard was fenced, and the gate was latched.

Max swooped into the yard and landed a safe distance from the bird, for he did not wish to be eaten. He gazed up at its massive head, wondering how the Great Gandor should be addressed. He had to make a good first impression, something he seldom did well. A rehearsal for the moment might have proved useful, but it had come upon him unexpected. He bowed to the bird.

'Good morning, Your Majesty. Am I addressing the Great Gandor?'

Max waited for a reply, hoping that the Great Gandor was not seeing him as a meal. The bird looked down, puzzled, and then he spoke.

'I don't think so. That is, not that I can remember. What is your name?'

Max was relieved by the non-threatening tone. 'My name is Max, Your Majesty, and I am looking for my sister, Alice.'

The bird's eyes lit up. 'I remember Alice. She told me that she had a brother called Max. Do you know him?'

'I am Max. Can you tell me where I can find her?' Max was excited.

The bird paused, scratched the ground, looked around, and then looked back at Max. 'What were we just talking about?' he asked in a vague tone.

'Alice!' squawked Max, and then he remembered that he was talking to the Great Gandor. Loud squawking was not a good idea. 'Sorry, Your Majesty, we were talking about Alice,' he said, trying to appear humble.

The bird paused again, scratched some more, and then said, 'I forget. I forget things all the time.'

A Sheep had wandered up to the yard and was listening from the other side of the fence. The giant bird shouted to the Sheep, 'Hey, Bruce, can you help my friend?'

The Sheep yelled back in a gravelly tone. 'Garry, my name is Garry. We have this same conversation every morning, Lofty.'

Max looked at the bird. The Sheep had called him Lofty, not Gandor.

'Is your name Lofty?' Max asked, but it was Garry who answered the question.

'You are talking to Lofty the Lost, the world's most forgetful Emu. Sometimes, he remembers everything, and the next moment, nothing. He has been that way ever since he fell on his head.'

'I thought Lofty was the Great Gandor,' Max explained, hoping that Garry could help, but Garry was no help at all.

'Lofty, not likely, and who the heck is the Great Gandor?'

Garry's grumpy manner was quickly eroding Max's optimism. He switched the conversation to Alice.

'I was asking Lofty about my sister, Alice, but then he forgot what he was going to say. Can you tell me anything about my sister?'

'Nope, don't know her.'

'She was going to see the Great Gandor.'

'I told you, I don't know him either.'

Then Lofty interrupted, for he had remembered something. 'Yes you can, Bruce. Alice goes by another name now.'

'Garry, my name is Garry, not Bruce, and I have no idea what you are talking about, Lofty.'

Lofty was adamant. 'But you do, the other name, you remember.'

Garry frowned. 'No idea.'

Lofty went on. 'I told you about her new name. The one the little bird told me about.'

Garry shrugged. 'I Don't know.'

Lofty frowned. 'Bruce, you have a shocking memory.'

Garry shook his head and walked away. Then he stopped and turned to Max.

'Follow me. Skippy will be along shortly. You can ask him.'

Lofty watched them leave, and then he remembered. *Dove Girl, that's it. Everyone calls her Dove Girl.* 'Bruce,' he shouted, but Garry and Max were already out of earshot.

31

GARRY THE GRUMPY SHEEP

Max was eager to ask Garry questions, but he found it difficult to keep pace. If he walked, Garry was too fast, and if he flew, Garry was too slow. Then he had an idea.

'Can I hitch a ride on your back?' he asked.

'You can try,' grunted Garry, 'but I bet you can't stay on.'

Max was up for the challenge. He hopped onto Garry's back and sank his claws deep into thick wool.

'Hang on,' yelled Garry as he broke into a gallop.

That's not fair, thought Max. *He was just trotting before.*

Max held on because a true adventurer never gives up, but his questions would have to wait until Garry stopped running.

Garry headed for a stand of tall gums that stood in the middle of a wide expanse of open ground. A short distance away, a gathering of Garry's friends grazed on stunted grass. Max felt immediate concern for the Sheep, for the whole area was surrounded by a wire fence strung between posts. The Sheep were prisoners, just like Lofty, but theirs was a much larger prison. It was a prison none the less.

Garry's gallop ended at the trees. 'I am not as fit as I used to be,' he panted.

Max hopped to the ground. 'That was fun for me, but you didn't have to run.'

Garry puffed some more and then bleated, 'I was trying to shake you off, but you were holding on too darn tight.'

Max waited for Garry to regain his breath, wondering how best to handle his grumpy attitude.

'Is Lofty a Penguin?' Max asked, for he had been wondering about Lofty's tiny wings.

Garry gave Max a long and enquiring look. *This is the craziest Magpie I have ever met,* he thought. 'No,' he said. 'I told you, Lofty is

111

an Emu. Don't you ever listen?' Garry thought some more. 'What is a Penguin, anyway, some friend of the Great Gandor, perhaps?'

Max explained how Penguins came from a land of frozen water, and that they swam everywhere because their wings were too tiny for flight.

Nebby would have been proud to hear Max tell the story, but Garry thought it was the greatest load of rubbish he had ever heard. He was wondering if Max had escaped from somewhere and guards would be coming along shortly to take him back. 'Stay here and look around,' he said, his voice suddenly calmer. Garry thought that calm was the best way to deal with a troubled person, but calmness was not in his nature, and Max's next words soon had him grumpy again.

'You live in a very spacious park,' said Max.

It was then that Garry saw the reason for Max to be an odd ball. 'You must be a city boy,' he growled.

Max felt offended. No one had ever called him a city boy before. He was a creature of the Natural World, not a city boy. 'What makes you say that?' he asked.

Garry looked about. 'Around here, we call this a paddock, not a park. You need to learn the language if you want to get on with us country people.'

Max was perplexed to hear that there were differences between city people and country people. 'What's wrong with city people? Aren't we all the same?' he asked.

Garry laughed, but it was not a happy laugh, and his gravelly voice gave dire meaning to his next words. 'City people never worry about the things that country people worry about, which means country people often suffer from what city people do.'

Garry is a hard bloke to cheer up, thought Max, and so he asked, 'How come city people do bad things that hurt country people?'

Garry frowned as if Max was the guilty party. 'City people don't worry about things outside their city because they have turned their back on Mother Nature's world.'

Max was not sure how to respond. He had never turned his back on Mother Nature, and he had never done anything to hurt country people. He looked to a branch above his head. 'I think I will take time out in this tree,' he said.

'Okay,' said Garry. 'I will give you a call if I see Skippy coming.'

32

SKIPPY

Max perched in the tree, keeping a watchful eye on Garry, for all the Sheep in the paddock looked the same. Fortunately, and perhaps not surprisingly, the other Sheep seemed happy to let Garry graze alone.

Suddenly, Max saw danger. An animal as large as Lofty was charging towards them. It had powerful hind legs and a long tail, and it bounded in mighty leaps. This time, it had to be the Great Gandor, and Garry was about to be eaten.

There was no time to think, no time to shout a warning, for Garry would never make it back to the safety of the other Sheep in time. Max had to stop the animal with the only weapon he had, his Magpie swoop.

'Run Garry!' he squawked as he launched himself from the tree. Unfortunately, squawking was a bad idea.

A feature of the Magpie swoop is its element of surprise. It is a silent attack, the victim knowing nothing until it happens. But Max's attack was no surprise. The bounding beast heard the squawk and looked up to see a black and white missile headed directly at him. Meanwhile, Garry, for whom the warning was meant, just kept on chewing grass.

It was then that Max realised that the lack of surprise was not his only problem, for something occurred to him as he closed in on his target. This was the first time that he had ever swooped an enemy. He had seen his father swoop Pastor Smith, but this victim was bounding. Max wondered what safety margin was required for such a target. He did not want the outcome to be an unfortunate clash of heads, and so he erred on the side of safety.

Max's inaugural swoop was little more than a gentle fly-over, the bounding beast not breaking stride as Max passed overhead. The beast continued onward until he reached Garry.

Max banked back and swooped to the ground, landing a safe distance away. He glared at the beast, letting him know that the fight was not yet over, but the beast took no notice. Garry took no notice either. He just kept on chewing, and then the beast spoke.

'Hi, Grumpy. Still dining with all your friends, I see.'

Max felt a sudden relief. *They know each other,* he thought, *but doesn't anybody ever call Garry by his proper name?*

Garry stopped chewing and looked up. 'Good day, Skippy. Still can't hop backwards, I notice.'

Oops, thought Max. *This is Skippy. I think I have just made another bad first impression.*

Skippy glanced at Max and then turned back to Garry. 'Who's the crazy Magpie, a friend of yours, I suppose?'

Garry chomped on another tuft of grass and then answered, his mouth half full.

'Not really. His name is Max, and I found him over at Lofty's, looking for his sister. I told him you might be able to help.'

Skippy turned to Max. 'Does your sister look like you?' he asked.

Garry interrupted. 'You will have to speak slower. Max is a city boy.'

Skippy laughed. 'That's a bit harsh, Garry.'

'Not really,' said Garry. 'I told him that we were waiting for someone called Skippy, but he never figured out that you were a Kangaroo.'

Skippy looked at Max. 'Is that right?'

'I had never seen a Kangaroo or a Sheep before today,' Max confessed.

'Oh dear,' said Skippy, 'you must be a city boy, and I suppose your sister looks just like you?'

'She does,' said Max, trying to sound polite.

Skippy shrugged. 'Don't think I can help you then. All Magpies look alike to me.'

This was not the answer Max wanted. 'She was going to see the Great Gandor,' he said.

Skippy shrugged again. 'I can't help you there either. I have never heard of the Great Gandor. Got any useful information?'

'She is looking for the Great River,' Max said in desperation.

Skippy shrugged a third time. 'Sorry, still can't help you. What is the Great River?'

'It is the place where many types of birds and animals gather,' Max explained.

Skippy's ears pricked up. 'Why didn't you say that in the first place? I can help you with that.'

'You can?'

Skippy smiled. 'A Magpie was here some time back. She was looking for a place like that and so I took her there.'

'That would have to be Alice,' Max squawked.

Skippy gave a grin. 'Follow me, city boy. We will go and find your sister.'

Skippy turned to Garry as they went to leave. 'See you tomorrow, Grumpy.'

Garry stopped munching. 'Not if I see you first and do something about that limp. It's about time you learnt to walk like a normal person.'

Max was surprised by their departing words and thought that he needed to say something more gracious. 'Thank you, Garry,' he squawked, 'I'm off to find my sister, Alice.'

'Whatever,' Garry mumbled as he went on chewing grass.

'Does he mind you calling him Grumpy,' Max asked Skippy once they were on their way.

Skippy laughed. 'I only call him Grumpy on his good days. Most days, I call him Chuckles.'

Country people can be very rude to each other, thought Max. He never wanted to be rude to anyone, but it sometimes just happened. However, country people seemed to do it on purpose.

'Sorry about the swoop,' Max said.

Skippy laughed again. 'If that was a swoop, then I think you should work on it. The flies around here are doing a better job than you.'

No more was said. The two continued, Skippy bounding over fences and bushes, and anything that got in the way. Max flew a safe distance above, avoiding Skippy's erratic bounds.

33

THE WELL-MEANING WILDLIFE PARK

The cross-country travellers reached the top of a hill beyond which lay a broad valley.

'We will stop here for a rest,' said Skippy, much to Max's relief, for his wings were beginning to tire.

He perched on a fence post, one of the countless fence posts that he had been seeing all morning. He was coming to the conclusion that Humans were fixated with putting up fences. Back home, they made them from sheets of metal, while in the country, they simply stuck posts in the ground and strung wire between them. It was pointless vandalism on a massive scale, because it robbed Mother Nature's creatures of their freedom. It made them prisoners in the paddocks in which they grazed. Only the birds were left free to roam.

'Why have the Humans put up all these fences?' Max asked.

Skippy did his usual laugh. 'The Humans put them up because they want to control the Natural World, but they can't control me.'

'Me neither,' said Max, who regarded himself as a Magpie adventurer.

Skippy chuckled. 'Right you are. The Humans may think that they can conquer Mother Nature's creatures, but we are warriors, and we will never surrender.'

'But keeping animals as prisoners is a bad thing,' Max said. 'Why are Humans so bad?'

Skippy grinned. 'I think you are going to love where I am taking you. It is a place where Mother Nature's creatures keep the Humans as slaves.'

Max was stunned into silence as he imagined how such a place could exist. Skippy continued to explain. The Well-meaning Wildlife Park was where he had taken Alice. It was a true gathering place of birds and animals, and they kept the Humans as slaves. The slaves brought the park residents their food, their drink, and made them shelters. Everyone lived a life of pampered luxury in the park.

This unexpected situation caused Max to think once more about the one case the detective within him was yet to solve. *Are Humans good or bad people?* Perhaps country Humans were different to city Humans. The singing Humans he had come across might be Mother Nature's good ones, and the slaves were the bad ones that she was still training. This she could do in the country because the outdoors was her realm, but she had no power over the Humans in the city. It was a good theory, but he needed more evidence before he could close the case.

Max wondered why the Crows had never told Nebby about the slaves being at the Great River, and then he thought how he had once scoffed at his sister for wanting to see the world. Her determination had led them to a paradise of ultimate justice. But then another question occurred to him. He looked at Skippy. 'Why don't you live in the park?' he asked.

Skippy stood tall, straightened his back, and he held his head high.

'I am a renegade. I lead a life of freedom. There are too many rules in the park, and rules are for weakies. I make my own rules.' Then he added, 'Come on, we are almost there. You can make up your own mind about the place.'

Skippy bounded on and Max followed. The valley was full of trees and bushes, unlike the open paddocks they had been seeing all morning, and as they descended into the valley, Max began to hear different birdcalls. Then came the odour of various animals, all mixed together, giving confusing clues about who lay ahead. The Great River had to be close, and so Max asked, 'Is there a river ahead?'

'No, just a pond,' Skippy answered.

The answer was not what Max expected to hear, but then they came upon a fence of wire netting. It was too high for Skippy to jump, but it had an opening through which passed a narrow road.

'They leave the gate open during the day,' Skippy said as he bounded through.

Max followed, and suddenly, he was in a strange, new world. It was a true gathering place of Mother Nature's creatures. He looked about in astonishment. *Everyone must have relatives here*, he thought. Flitting between the treetops were coloured birds that were the same as those that sometimes visited Gum Tree Park. In one tree, Max saw Charlie's relatives, their vivid white plumage standing out against the soft green leaves of the gum. In another, he saw someone who could easily have been mistaken for Nebby, hunched motionless, high in the branches. Then Max heard a familiar tweet and saw relatives of Tinker and Tinkalina hopping around on the ground. Then a relative of Lofty ran by.

However, nothing could have prepared Max for his next shock, for not far from the gate was a bale of hay, and it was being demolished by a monster. A great, brown beast, with a long neck, long legs, oversized feet, and a humped back, was chewing on a mouthful of straw. Dwarfed alongside the monster was a Human, dressed in brown trousers and a dark green top.

'What's that?' gasped Max, staring at the monster.

'That's a Human slave. All slaves are dressed that way so that we can tell that they are slaves.'

Skippy delighted in giving park visitors their first view of a Human slave, but he was a poor guide and seldom answered the actual question being asked.

'Not the Human, the monster next to him. It has to be the Great Gandor,' Max squawked.

Skippy chuckled. 'You need to get over this thing you have about the Great Gandor. He does not exist. Are you not amazed by what the slave is doing?'

Max was relieved to see that Skippy was not concerned about the monster, whose vegetarian diet suggested that he did not eat people. However, that also meant that he was not the Great Gandor.

'You mean scooping up that animal's poop and putting it in the wheelbarrow?' Max asked.

'Yes,' said Skippy. 'You don't see animals doing that sort of thing for Humans.'

'No,' said Max, 'but who is the animal that is making the poop in the first place?'

Skippy was disappointed, for Max had returned to a boring question about a Camel.

'Oh, that's Kevin the Camel. Some people around here say that Camels should not be in the park because they are immigrants, but I think they make the place more interesting.'

Just then, another Camel trotted up and began chewing the hay.

'And who is that?' exclaimed Max, taking a backward step.

'That's another Kevin the Camel,' said Skippy, hoping for more slave questions, not Camel questions. However, he already knew what the next question would be, and so he went on. 'There are rules around here that you might find strange.'

'What sort of rules?' Max asked.

Skippy rolled his eyes. 'Rules you will have to get used to, and oh, by the way, no one is called Max around here. Your name is Maggie.'

Max was both puzzled and annoyed, for Skippy's skills as an informative guide needed improving. 'How come I am no longer Max?' he squawked.

Skippy gave another chuckle. 'Don't worry about it, Maggie, I will get someone to explain the whole place to you later.'

The news of another guide was good to hear, for Max had many questions and Skippy's cryptic answers were not helping. Maggie was a girl's name, something he would have to impress on whomever would be his guide. However, he had one question which he hoped Skippy could answer.

'What will the Human do with the poop?' he asked.

Skippy shook his head. 'One can only wonder. The Human tips it onto the back of his truck and takes it home. What he does with it then is a mystery no one likes to think about, let alone solve.'

Max was contemplating the possible uses for a pile of poop when a lady Kangaroo bounded up to them.

34

THE LAND OF EQUAL OPPORTUNITY

The lady Kangaroo appeared pleased to see Skippy, so pleased in fact that she did not notice Max standing there. He had to hop to one side to avoid being whacked by the sweep of her tail.

'Hello Skippy,' said Skippy.

'Hello Skippy,' said she.

Max looked up at the lady Kangaroo. 'Are you both called Skippy?' he asked.

The lady Kangaroo wondered where the voice had come from, and then she spied Max. Embarrassed, with not having seen him before, she went into a lengthy answer.

'Yes, but my folks actually called me George when I was born because they guessed that I was a boy. You must realise that many babies are too small for parents to know what they are when they are born. Half the people around here started life with the wrong name, but they have fixed all that. All Kangaroos are now called Skippy.'

Max hoped that Ms Skippy was not the one intended as his guide, for her answers were just as confusing as Mr Skippy's, only hers were longer.

'Who has fixed what?' Max asked, once Ms Skippy had stopped to take a breath.

Ms Skippy continued, and she spoke with pride. 'The Committee for Animal Equality has made a special rule. All animals of the same species must have the same name. It is an excellent rule.'

'Do you really think so?' said Max, but Ms Skippy was not about to doubt her answer.

'Of course, it is. I know that your name is Maggie even though we have never been formally introduced. Heaven forbid, gone are the embarrassing days of getting people's names wrong.'

'Surely not everyone agrees with that rule?' asked a doubtful Max.

Ms Skippy frowned. 'Some troublemakers have been evicted in the past. There was an Emu here once who could never remember people's names and thought that his name was Lofty. We evicted him because noncompliance of the rules is the path that leads to lawlessness.'

'Poor Lofty, cast out because of a rule,' Max said.

Ms Skippy appeared shocked. 'It is a wonderful rule, and no one should ever criticise the work of the committee. Even our Human slaves abide by their rules.'

'Really?' said Max.

'Yes, they call each other Mate.' Ms Skippy folded her front legs to make her answer sound more emphatic.

Mr Skippy interrupted. 'I could stand here all day listening to you two going on, but I think I need to be finding something more interesting to do.'

Ms Skippy appeared alarmed. 'Oh no, don't go yet. We haven't had a chance to chat.'

Max could see that three was a crowd, and he was number three. He excused himself.

'I will just be over there chasing worms or whatever,' he said. 'You guys chat, and thanks for your help, Mr Skippy. I will get Ms Skippy to show me around after you have gone.'

The two Skippys chatted for some time while Max did his best to harass worms. Finally, Mr Skippy left. Max flew over to join Ms Skippy as she wistfully watched Mr Skippy bound away.

'You have to watch that one,' she said. 'He's a bit of a rogue.'

'Why do I have to watch him?' Max asked.

Ms Skippy laughed. 'Actually, you don't, but I do.'

Max felt uncomfortable with that answer. 'Would you be able to show me around now?' he asked.

Ms Skippy returned to her more talkative self. 'Certainly, follow me. You have many people to meet, but don't worry, you won't have trouble remembering their names.'

Max's grand tour took up the rest of the day, and he was astonished by the variety of creatures living in the park. Between each new encounter, Ms Skippy explained another park rule. Finally, Max's head was spinning, for there were far too many rules for him to remember. However, the fighting rule was one that did stick.

'No one is allowed to fight for food or territory,' Ms Skippy warned. 'Troublemakers found guilty of such an offence, are either locked up or banished.'

'You have a prison?' Max asked.

'Oh yes,' Ms Skippy said in her elegant tone, 'but I thought that I would introduce you to all the nice people first. You can see where we keep the prisoners tomorrow.'

The advanced society of the park was what Alice had hoped to find at the Great River. Creatures of many kinds had come together to share wisdom and knowledge. They lived lives of luxury, under rules that guaranteed peace and harmony. However, to Max, it felt wrong. *How can creatures enjoy Mother Nature's world if they are stuck here living under rules?* he thought. This place could not be the Great River because there was no river, and then he wondered, *Where is Alice?*

'Where is Alice, my sister?' Max asked.

Ms Skippy frowned, something she did well. 'We have no Magpie here called Alice. As I have already explained to you, we only have Magpies called Maggie.'

Max decided that rather than argue, he would look for Alice later, for there was something else that made him curious.

'Why doesn't Mr Skippy live in the park?' he asked.

Ms Skippy sighed. 'Unfortunately, park life does not suit the free spirit of my renegade.'

Somehow, Max found himself siding with the feelings of the renegade Skippy.

35

A FAMILY REUNION

It was almost dusk by the time Max finished his tour. The final stop was the tree allocated for Magpies to roost. Several of them were gathered under the tree, all hoeing into a bowl of food left by the slaves.

'You have to stay with the other Magpies,' Ms Skippy said as she went to leave.

'Thank you,' said Max, but Ms Skippy did not acknowledge. She hopped away without saying goodbye. 'Maybe my manners aren't so bad after all,' Max mumbled.

He wandered over to the other Magpies. 'Hi everyone, my name is Max.'

The Magpies stopped eating and looked at him. 'No one is called Max around here,' said one.

'If you break the rules, we will have to ask you to leave,' said another.

Max was not prepared to argue. He was more interested in having something to eat.

'What is the pecking order around here?' he asked, wondering how long he would have to wait for a meal.

An elderly Magpie stepped up. 'The rules have banned the eating by pecking order, and besides, the slaves bring us so much food that we don't need one.'

'So, anyone called Maggie can eat first,' Max joked, but no one laughed.

Sullen lot, he thought. *I guess I just go and help myself.*

Max examined the contents of the bowl, an odd mixture of mash, meat, and bugs. He picked out some bugs and bits of meat, but he left the mash because it was not his type of food.

Once having eaten, he asked, 'Are there any other Magpies in the park apart from you guys?'

The elderly Magpie answered. 'There is one other who is in jail, but no one is permitted to associate with prisoners.'

That prisoner has to be Alice, thought Max, and he let out a loud squawk. 'Where do I find the jail?'

Max's manner startled the group, for aggression was not permitted in the park. The elderly Magpie quickly pointed the way, but he warned that it was breaking the rules to go there. Max ignored the warning and headed for the jail.

In the corner of the park stood a collection of wire cages. At first glance, they all appeared empty with their doors wide open. However, he then noticed that one door was closed, but that cage also appeared to be empty. Max landed on top of the closed cage so that he could better see inside. He peered down through the wire.

At first, he saw nothing, but as his eyes became accustomed to the dim light, he saw someone hiding in the corner. A small patch of white moved in the shadows. Max stared at the patch and realised that he was looking at the back of a Magpie.

The hiding Magpie could hide no longer, and so he spoke. 'Is that you, Squirt?'

The feeble voice hit Max with a wave of disbelief. 'Brian! Is that you, Brian?'

'Sure is, Squirt. What's new?'

Max could not believe it. Brian, the nemesis of his childhood, the one destined to lead, the bully who never paid attention in class, the brother everyone thought was dead. Brian was cowering in the corner, a victim of an abduction, just like Dopey, only Dopey had managed to escape. Max needed to think. He had to get his brother out of there, but night was fast closing. Then he realised that there were people who could help, but he had to be quick.

'Don't worry,' whispered Max, 'I met some Cockatoos this afternoon. They are experts at undoing latches. If I go now, I can catch them before they turn in. We will get you out of here.'

'No, I don't want to come out. It is a dangerous world out there.'

Brian sounded frightened, and Max had once heard another bird say almost the same thing. Charlie had said that it was an unfriendly world out there, and he would not come out of his cage either. Max wondered if both birds had been brain washed by the Humans.

Were Humans good or bad people? The same question was haunting him again. He had been thinking that the park slaves would do no harm to Mother Nature's creatures because she was training them, yet they were doing harm to Brian. Perhaps Mother Nature's ways were simply too hard for a Magpie to fathom.

Max remained perched where he was, and the two brothers chatted as darkness fell, just as they had once done back in their student dormitory. However, Max decided to hold back the story of Alice being thrown out of home. He thought it best that he only tell happy stories, and besides, Alice's fate would probably delight his callous brother.

Brian had never met the people at Gum Tree Park, for he had been abducted before he could fly. Max decided to tell him about them, starting with Nebby. However, typical of Brian, he scoffed at Max's description of a Koala being wise and spending the day deep in thought.

'Koalas don't think all day, they just sleep, and they know nothing about science,' he said.

Max froze upon hearing the word, 'science'. His detective mind raced. *I didn't say that Nebby was a scientist. Brian would only know that if someone from home had told him. Brian has spoken to Alice.*

'Alice has been to see you,' Max squawked. Up until then, he had been speaking quietly, although he was not sure why.

However, Brian's voice remained soft. 'Don't worry about her, Squirt, I will tell you about her later. I want my questions answered first.'

'No, tell me about her now,' Max shouted.

'No, Squirt. You tell me about Mum and the others. I am keeping my story about Alice until you have told me everything I want to know.'

He was still the same old Brian, doing whatever he could to feel superior. Max had no choice. He told Brian about their parents, Nebby, Dopey, Charlie, and all the others. Finally, there was no one left to talk about. It was time to talk about Alice.

Max asked the question once more. 'Tell me, where is Alice?'

Brian's voice remained soft. 'Maxie, everyone thinks that our sister is dead.'

Brian had never called him Maxie before. Alice was the one who called him Maxie. It could mean only one thing; Brian truly believed that Alice was dead. Max's heart sank, but a glimmer of hope still floated, for it takes a lot to sink the spirit of an adventurer.

'Are you telling me that no one knows for sure?' Max squawked.

Brian gazed out through the wire that held him prisoner. 'She never came back.'

'Came back from where?'

Brian then told Max how Alice had come to the park, thinking that it might be the mythical Great River. She stayed for some time but was disillusioned by the park's rules and lack of freedom. When someone told her about the Lookout, a dead tree that sits on the highest point in the land, she had to go there. She thought it might be a place from where she could see the Great River in the distance. But foolishly, she ignored the warnings about the Lookout.

'What warnings?'

Brian went on. 'There are many stories about the Lookout, but none can be verified, for no one has ever come back.'

'So, did she go?' asked Max.

'She did,' said Brian, 'and some people were pleased to see her leave.'

'Why?' asked Max, whose dislike for the park and its rules was beginning to grow.

Brian paused, for the answer required him to tell of his sister's fame, which was something that had annoyed him. However, he had no choice other than to tell the story.

'Alice had become a celebrity,' he said. 'She performed a flying trick not done by Magpies, and people gave her a special name, but special names were banned under the rules.'

'What special name?' Max asked.

Brian laughed. 'It was a stupid name. They called her Dove Girl.'

'That would have been because of the flying trick that she learnt from Dopey,' Max said.

'Makes sense,' said Brian, 'but no one can rise above the rest around here. Alice infuriated the committees.'

'Did Alice ever talk about finding the Great Gandor?' Max asked, changing the subject.

Brian shook his head. 'Alice said that she had given up looking for the Great Gandor. Nebby told her that he was a legend, but no one around here has ever heard of him. Alice guessed that Nebby was confusing his facts with his fiction, and she blamed his gum leaf diet.'

'It looks like I will have to go to the Lookout,' said Max, his voice gripped with determination.

'You won't come back,' warned Brian.

The conversation fell silent. Max looked towards the moon. Nearby, a lone Owl sat listening, a cricket chirped, and in the distance, relatives of Willy partied. All else was quiet, but out there somewhere, was Alice.

Brian's words ran through his head. *You won't come back.* They burned in his brain. Brian was the bully from his past, but he was now afraid of his own shadow. Brian would never again tell him that he was not good enough. He was going to find Alice or die in the quest. He glared down through the mesh of the cage and squawked, 'Tell me, how do I get to the Lookout.'

36

THE LOOKOUT

Max woke early the next morning and found the park to be alive with activity. The Magpies were leading the singing of a morning chorus, assisted by Kookaburras and other birds, with the Ducks adding the occasional quack as they wandered down to the pond. Ms Skippy stood chatting with the park's Kangaroos, and all seemed to have their eyes fixed on a hut not far from the gate. A short time later, a slave emerged from the hut and began dispensing food, causing everyone to rush to their appointed eating places.

No hunting here, thought Max. *Food comes served by the slaves. No wonder Mr Skippy says that they are all weakies.*

The slave stopped at Brian's cage, looked up, and spotted Max.

'Oh, I see, you have a friend. Come on down and have some breakfast.'

The slave placed food on the ground for Max. He then opened the cage door, reached in, and put food in a bowl for Brian.

'Come out and play with your friend,' he said, but Brian did not move.

'Suit yourself; I will leave the door open as usual. One of these days you will decide that it is safe to come out.'

Once the slave was gone, Max flew down to inspect the food. He thought that Brian would join him, but his brother remained where he was.

'Come out. We can go and find Alice together,' Max said. Max thought it would be great to have his brother share his adventure.

'I will never come out,' said Brian. 'I told you, it is a dangerous world out there. If you had any sense, you would live in here with me. If you don't, you will be sorry, and one day soon I will hear about your horrible death.'

Brian was never a cheery person at breakfast, and Max realised that he was better off without him. A negative thinker was not needed on his adventure. He finished his breakfast, said goodbye, and set out to find the Lookout.

Max flew hard that day and was close to exhaustion when he first glimpsed his destination. It appeared in the distance, the skeletal remains of a dead tree that stood atop the summit of the tallest hill. The hill was barren except for that dead tree, and even from a distance, the tree had an eerie aura. However, Max was too tired to go on, so he found a comfortable bush to rest for the night, but he did not sleep well. He was worried about the day to come.

He woke the next morning to the sound of distant carolling, and he wondered if he would ever hear those wonderful voices again. According to Brian, this day would probably be his last, and so he foraged for a breakfast befitting that of a doomed person, and luck was with him. He found a succulent feast hiding under a pile of animal dung, and he dined like a king.

Once having dined, he set forth to his daunting destination, the place from which no one had ever returned. By mid-day, he had reached the foot of the hill. He paused and looked upward. Above stood the tree, rigid and ghostly, its dead limbs reaching to the sky.

Max took a deep breath and began the steep flight to the summit. After several rests, he made it to the tree and was surprised to find that its limbs had been partly blackened by fire. He perched on one of the blackened branches, but it was not a good day for viewing. The Great River could well have been in sight, but a misty haze cloaked the distant horizon.

He began to feel nervous but could see nothing that could harm him. His positive spirit told him that the committees had probably made up the frightening stories to stop people leaving the park.

Then Max looked down to the ground and noticed that it was littered with small, white stones. Like a true detective, he had to investigate. He flew down, but to his horror, he discovered that they were not stones—they were bones. A chill told him to flee, but the warning came too late. Beneath him should have been his shadow, but it was gone, enveloped by the much larger shadow of something hovering behind him. He froze as powerful claws wrapped around his body.

'Gotcha, my fine feathered, midday snack.'

Max was stunned but could only listen. His captor's grip held him powerless, unable to turn his head. Strangely, the gloating voice did not sound frightening, but the words, 'midday snack', made up for that. A question ran through Max's mind. *Is this how my great adventure ends?*

It was a strange thing to be thinking, but Max felt powerless, for his fate was inevitable. He answered his own question. *Probably*. Then he thought what he thought would be the last thought that he would ever think. *I wonder what Alice is doing right now?*

Max could hear the pounding of his heart as he waited for the final blow, but then his captor began to mutter. 'Only a stupid bird would come up here.'

Max assumed that his captor was talking to himself, but he answered anyway. 'I came here looking for someone.'

'Quiet,' said his captor.

The sharp tone left Max in no doubt. He had to be quiet, for he was not the one being spoken to, but so what, it was not as though his captor could threaten to kill him or something. 'I am looking for the Great Gandor,' Max squawked.

It might have made more sense for Max to have said that he was looking for Alice, but somehow, his current situation brought the Great Gandor to mind.

'Who?' said his captor.

Max's captor had spoken again, but this time, it appeared that he was asking Max a question. A few more moments had been added to Max's life.

'The Great Gandor,' Max gasped. 'The legend. The one who sees all.'

Max's captor released his grip and resumed his mumbling. 'Darn, this is what comes from talking to your food. My mother always told me, "Never talk to your food". Now look what has happened.'

Max struggled to his feet and turned to face the person about to eat him. There stood a magnificent Eagle.

Had a Cat like Felix stood in Max's place, he would have run in terror, for a Cat would have been no match for the Eagle's massive talons. A Cat would have been ripped apart and a powerful beak would have chewed him to pieces. Max stood in awe as he gathered his wits. 'Mine too,' he said, remembering the things his mother had taught him, and about the time when Herbert had met his sudden demise.

'Really?' said the Eagle.

'Really,' said Max. 'We got into trouble if we talked to our food.'

But it was not mother's rules that had upset the Eagle's dinner plans. 'Tell me, why do you seek the Great Gandor?' he asked.

No one had ever asked Max that question before. Everyone simply told him that the Great Gandor did not exist. Max wondered if the Eagle knew something that no one else knew.

'I need to ask the Great Gandor a question. Do you know where I can find him?'

The Eagle posed as Albert often posed when giving his king of the bush speech. In a majestic voice, he spoke.

'You are looking at the Great Gandor.'

'Really?' said Max.

'Really,' said the Great Gandor.

'But nobody around here knows that you exist?' Having said these words, Max thought that he might have blundered once more, for he never made a good first impression.

The Great Gandor looked away and sighed. 'They call me the Evil Eagle around here. No one knows me as the Great Gandor anymore. You are never a prophet in your own parish.'

'You are a legend where I come from,' said Max, hoping to win favour.

'Really,' said the Great Gandor.

'Really,' said Max.

'But why did you come here looking for me?' The curiosity of the Great Gandor had been aroused.

'I was told that my sister, Alice, came up here, and I am actually looking for her.'

The Great Gandor looked at the scattered bones. 'Sorry, but I never ask their names.'

The Gandor's sheepish tone said it all, and Max was horrified. He looked at the bones, hoping he would not see a Magpie's skull. The Gandor sensed his anxiety.

'I don't eat every Magpie I meet, you know. Some time back, that special Magpie came to see me. She was a lovely girl, and we talked for ages.'

'What special Magpie?' Max asked.

'The one they call Dove Girl. She is a legend, and I am a legend, and it is bad luck for a legend to eat a legend.'

The superstition that surrounded legend eating was music to Max's ears. Alice was still alive.

'Dove Girl is my sister. What became of her?' Max squawked.

The Gandor thought back, recalling Alice's visit. He told Max that he sometimes found it difficult to remember past events.

Nothing was said for a while, which gave Max time to again examine the bones of the Gandor's victims. The Gandor then spoke.

'I remember,' he said. 'I told her about a Magpie settlement that takes in stray Magpies. I sometimes drop in there for a meal because it is close by. I think that is where she went.'

'What do you normally eat there?' Max asked.

The Gandor laughed. 'Let us just say that every time I leave, they have room to take in one more stray.'

The Gandor's laugh brought Max back to reality, for there was still an important matter to be settled. 'I wonder if you would kindly forgo your midday snack and let me be on my way?' Max asked.

The Gandor laughed again. 'Seeing that I am not hungry, I excuse you from your responsibility to be my meal. Be my guest instead. Stay the night, and we will talk about all the things that our mothers told us. I can offer you some nice bugs that live under the stones over there.'

Max was overjoyed, as he reflected on the alternative that could have been, but he thought it best not to show his relief. To be the guest of the Great Gandor was an honour he could never have imagined, an experience that he wished he could one day boast about to Nebby.

37

BERNARD

That afternoon, the Gandor went for a joy flight while Max rested after his long journey. He watched the Gandor circling effortlessly above, held high aloft by rising thermals. *I now know why they say he sees all,* thought Max as he enjoyed his lesser view from the Lookout. He tried the Gandor's bugs and washed them down with cool water from a nearby rock pool. The meal was delicious.

The Gandor returned at dusk and the two exchanged stories of their childhood before turning in. Max woke the next morning just as the Gandor was about to set out once more.

'Wait,' Max cried, 'I have something I forgot to ask you,' but he was too late.

'Got to go,' said the Gandor. 'It's the early Eagle that catches the early bird.' He launched himself into the air and was gone.

'I thought it was the early bird that catches the worm,' Max muttered as he watched the Gandor fly away.

Max had forgotten to ask about the Great River, which meant he would have to stay until the Gandor returned. However, a second meeting might not work out as well as the first. Max considered the risks.

Alice was protected by the superstition that surrounded legend eating, but Max was not a legend. Then there was the risk of the Gandor having a poor day's hunting and arriving back still looking for supper. The Gandor also had memory issues and might forget that Max was his guest.

Max decided it best to leave, and he began what he thought would be the longest downward glide ever attempted by a Magpie. He aimed for the place where the Gandor had told him that there was a Magpie settlement. The glide felt exhilarating. From time to time, he had to bank to wipe off speed, and he could see why Alice loved her Dove

Dive. Then he thought about that idiot, Dopey. If Dopey had not taught Alice her Dove Dive, she would never have become a legend and they would both have ended up as Gandor food. However, Alice was a legend, and a legend leaves a trail that he can follow.

Dopey, you are not a bad bloke after all, Max thought.

Once back to normal altitude, he searched for a good hunting ground. He was hungry and a clearing with soft earth looked a good place to drop in for breakfast. *I should find a few worms there,* he thought, and he was right. The place was a worm gold mine, and they were all for him. He could not understand why other birds were not feasting there as well. However, Max's activities were being closely watched.

A large Magpie swooped in and stood on a nearby rock. Max's normal response would have been to greet the newcomer, but Max was dealing with a juicy worm that was squirming in his beak. The large Magpie spread his wings and squawked in a deep voice.

'I am Bernard, grand master of the Kingdom of Bernard. I command thee to drop thy worm.'

Very impressive entrance, thought Max, who thought it only polite to do as asked. He dropped the worm and it plopped to the ground, heartened by what had just happened.

Bernard continued. 'He who doth eat the worms of this place doth become food for the Devil.'

Bernard's words delighted the worm, but Max was not impressed. He thought that Bernard had an odd way of speaking, and so he humoured him.

'Why do you say only, "he". Doesn't the Devil like the taste of girls?'

The joke did not go well. Bernard took a deep breath. 'Do not mock my words. Long ago, the Devil ate but worms, but then other birds didst begin the eating of his worms. The Devil didst then forsake the eating of his worms and began the feasting on the flesh of birds instead. We leave these worms as offering, that the Devil might once more return to righteous eating.'

Righteous eating? thought the worm.

Impressive sermon, thought Max, but Bernard's pretentious attitude amused him.

'Has anyone ever talked this over with the Devil?' he asked.

Bernard spread his wings once more. 'The Devil doth live on yonder Lookout. He circles above and doth come to earth to feast on those who ignore my command. No one speaks to the Devil, for those who hath tried, hath all been eaten.'

Max laughed. 'You mean the Evil Eagle. I stayed with him last night. We had a nice long chat.'

Bernard flew into a rage. 'Then it is true what my followers doth tell me. Thou hath come down from the Lookout. Thou art in league with the Devil. Thou art like the other who didst come to us from Satan's Lair.'

Something was not adding up. How could Bernard say that someone had come from Satan's Lair after saying that Satan eats everyone who tries to speak to him? The guy was telling fibs.

'What other?' asked Max.

Bernard scowled and looked away. 'The Devil's Maiden who doth go by the name, Dove Girl. Like thou, she didst confess to conversing with the Bird of Darkness, and so my people cast the wicked witch into the wilderness.'

Max had a sudden impulse to whack Bernard right in the beak, but he held back, for he needed to know more.'

'To which direction didst thou cast the witch?' he asked. Max was beginning to speak like Bernard. It was contagious.

Bernard turned to the side. 'She hath doomed herself for her wicked ways, for she journeys in the direction from which the sun rises. She will awake one morning and be consumed in his furnace.'

Bernard flung his wing towards the horizon and thundered his final command. 'Be off thou son of Satan, be off.'

I guess that's it then, thought Max. *I will be off. The trail of the wicked witch may still be warm.*

As Max went to leave, a small voice chimed in. 'Well go on then, be off.'

You are one very lucky worm, thought Max.

As he launched himself into the air, that same voice gave a pitiful little cry. Max looked back. The worm was struggling in Bernard's beak. *Kingdoms are all alike,* Max mused to himself. *The rules never apply to the one who makes them.*

He flew high above the trees, did a full circle of Bernard's kingdom, gave its namesake one final gesture with the tip of his wing, and then set out into the wilderness.

38

INTO THE WILDERNESS

Max headed towards the place from where the sun rises. As the day drew on, he thought about Bernard's last words. Alice had been cast into the wilderness, and Max was beginning to see what that meant. The landscape was changing. What few trees there were, were all stunted and the grass was frail and yellow. A Magpie would never choose to live in such a place and being there made him anxious. Alice would only have come that way if told to by the Great Gandor.

He began to ponder on the possibility of perishing in such a wasteland. Vanished without a trace was an excellent fate for an adventurer, but it was not what he had in mind. He pushed on, hoping for better things ahead, and things did change, but not for the better.

Since leaving home, Max had known nothing but hills. He would fly over one hill only to find another hill hiding behind it. He had spent the whole journey flying over, around, and between hills. He had begun his journey in a lush gorge, but what he was seeing now was far from lush.

It was late in the day and Max had time to cross just one more hill. He flew to its summit, expecting to see another hill beyond, but the next hill was not there. Instead, a vast plain, carpeted with gaunt bushes and stunted trees, lay before him. He looked to the distance, hoping to see the Great River, but the plain went forever. He saw no birds, no animals, just thirsty scrub clutching for survival in parched ground.

He gasped at what he saw, and he thought about giving up. There was no way that a Magpie could survive in such a place. *Where would I find food, water, and shelter?* he asked himself. Then he thought about Alice. What had she done, for she must have faced the same problem? Did she continue, or did she change direction? If only he had asked the Great Gandor the way to the Great River. That way, he would know for sure what Alice had done. He thought about going back to ask, but that came with risks.

However, Max's current priority was to find water and a place to roost, and water was scarce in the barren hills. He looked around, wondering if it ever rained in the wilderness, and then he spied something he had seen once before at the wildlife park. People called it a windmill, and the windmill was where the slaves got their water. Max wondered if he might find water at this windmill.

39

HOMER

Max flew to the windmill, and sure enough, he found a trough full of water. As a bonus, the ground around the trough was moist and had attracted a host of little critters. *Supper*, he thought. He drank with relish and was about to harass his supper when he heard a voice.

'My guess is that you are lost,' said the voice.

Max turned, and there, perched high on the windmill, was a stupid Pigeon. Max knew that the Pigeon was stupid, because Dopey had told everyone that all Pigeons were stupid. To make matters worse, the Pigeon was roosting where Max had planned to roost. *What rotten luck,* he thought, *running into an idiot Pigeon in the middle of nowhere. I hope he is not a talker. I need my sleep.*

'What makes you think I'm lost?' said Max in an offhanded manner.

'Don't usually see Magpies around here.'

The Pigeon was stating the obvious because they were the only two birds in the area.

'I take it you're a local?' Max asked, not wishing to prolong the conversation.

'No, I am here because of a stupid mistake.' The Pigeon sounded annoyed.

At least this Pigeon knows he is stupid, Max mused to himself. *Perhaps his stupid mistake would be good for a laugh,* and so he asked, 'And what stupid mistake was that?'

The Pigeon shook his feathers. He was tired and annoyed, and he had not anticipated being disturbed in such an isolated place. He hesitated, hoping to avoid answering, but Max kept staring at him, expecting an answer.

The Pigeon let out a reluctant sigh. 'My name is Homer, and I am a Homing Pigeon. I have been the champion of many races.'

'My name is Max,' Max interrupted.

Homer went on. 'Hello, Max, now where was I. Oh yes, I remember. I was in a race and stupidly thought that I could cross the Mallee Plain without taking a drink. That is the plain that you can see down there.'

They looked down at the plain, now bathed in the glow of a crimson sunset. Homer shook his feathers once more. 'I have crossed that plain many times, but never in a drought year.'

'What is a drought year?' Max asked.

'It's a year when there isn't much rain.' Homer then stared at Max and said, 'You must be a city boy.'

Max shrugged. He was not getting into that conversation again, particularly with a stupid Pigeon.

Homer continued. 'There is only one watering place left on the Mallee Plain, but it is guarded by Crows, and they let no other birds drink there. Luckily, I am a champion flyer and made the crossing without stopping, but now I must rest. I have to start racing again first thing in the morning. If you plan to stay here tonight, please don't keep me awake with Magpie chatter.'

Max was offended. He was not a talker. He wanted his sleep too. He thought about snubbing Homer for his insult but was curious to know about the race.

'What happened to the others in your race?' he asked.

A more sensitive Magpie would have understood how much Homer needed to rest, but the adolescent Max was immature when it came to reading the feelings of others. He kept staring at Homer as he waited for an answer.

Homer groaned. 'Most of them would be close to home by now. I passed a bunch having a drink, but I did not stop. I stupidly thought it was my chance to get ahead, but flying on without taking that drink has exhausted me.'

Homer had had enough. He turned his back, hoping Max would get the hint, but subtle gestures never worked on Max. He wanted to know more.

'Where were they when you passed them?'

Homer groaned again. This was definitely the last question he would answer. He looked back over his shoulder. 'They were taking a drink at the Great River.'

Unwittingly, Homer had just blown any chance for a quiet night. An animated Max was suddenly in his face. 'Tell me, where is the Great River? I am looking for the Great River, but no one knows where it is.'

Max's squawks shattered Homer's drowsy state. 'I take it that you have never asked a Pigeon about the Great River?'

'No,' said Max, as he thought, *I was always told that Pigeons were too stupid to know anything.*

Homer drew a deep breath. 'Pigeons fly all over the world. Next time you want to know where a place is, you should ask a Pigeon.'

Max never knew that Pigeons were world travellers. He thought they preferred the safety of cages, like Charlie and Brian.

Homer went on, and he told Max that the Great River was on the far side of the Mallee Plain, but he would have to wait until rain filled the water holes before attempting a crossing. He explained that Pigeons were powerful, long-distance flyers, who could make the journey nonstop, but a Magpie would perish if it did not find water. He also told him that the windmill on which they perched, was a landmark that the Pigeons called the Wilderness Windmill.

Max now knew what he had to do. He would stay with the Wilderness Windmill until it rained, and then he would cross the Mallee Plain. Dopey had given him the wrong impression about Pigeons, for he now held them in high regard.

That night, Max roosted with his newfound hero.

40

TROUBLE BACK HOME

Max had no way of knowing how long he would have to wait at the windmill, nor did he know about the dramatic events that were unfolding back home. The citizens of Gum Tree were facing a dilemma, for a Magpie with a broken beak was swooping everyone who came to their park. Only Pastor Smith was not bothered, for he had begun the wearing of a broad brimmed hat to foil any Magpie attack. However, most were calling for the rogue bird to be shot, despite the pastor's appeal for tolerance.

'We must learn to live with Mother Nature's creatures,' he would plead. 'Swooping is seasonal, and the season will soon end.'

However, Albert's vendetta against Humans had continued long after the swooping season was over. It was his way of winning respect, not realising that even the Magpies saw his behaviour as irrational. Only Muriel came to his defence.

'We have to wait until Albert gets things out of his system,' she kept telling everyone.

'Gets what things out of his system?' they would ask.

To this, Muriel had no useful answer, but could only say, 'He won't say what it is that bothers him. If I knew, we might be able to help, but his pride gets in the way.'

All the while, the pastor kept going to the park, for it gave him inspiration for his sermons. He would sit on the park's seat, unperturbed by Albert glaring down at him. His broad brimmed hat made him safe, but Albert was ready to swoop should he ever take it off.

This tenuous relationship between man and bird might have continued indefinitely, had it not been for the annual Sunday school picnic. The picnic was always held in the park, but the parents worried that the coming picnic could see their children swooped. The pastor called a meeting and suggested that everyone wear a large hat, but the parents argued that keeping large hats on the heads of excited children was not possible. The pastor then suggested that the picnic be held in the church car park, but the parents would not compromise. A bird could not stop people doing what they wanted, and they would not listen when the pastor reasoned that people must learn to live with Mother Nature's creatures. They called for Albert's head.

Next morning, Pastor Smith went to the park and sat once more on the seat. The Magpie flock admired how he always came back, but this only added to Albert's anger. He would glare down from his throne, for he wanted the pastor gone and would not stop until he had made it happen. He planned an attack that would see his enemy injured, but the pastor was yet to remove his hat.

Albert took little notice when a police car arrived that morning. He also ignored the police officer who stepped out of the car, and he failed to see the rifle with a telescopic sight that the officer carried. The officer had orders to shoot the Magpie with the broken beak. He rested his rifle on the car's bonnet and took careful aim. Albert was perched less than 30 metres away and was focused on the pastor, imagining the damage his claws could inflict should the pastor reveal his bald head. However, the pastor was there on a mission of mercy. He knew that Albert was in grave danger that morning.

'Stop!' shouted the pastor.

The police officer did not respond, for concentration is needed when taking aim.

Albert's gaze remained on the pastor, who was now running towards the Magpie assassin, but in vain. The officer looked through the scope, fixed Albert in the cross hairs, and squeezed the trigger.

Perhaps it was divine intervention, who knows, but at that exact moment, the pastor's hat blew off. At last, Albert saw his chance. He leaned forward as the rifle cracked, and a bullet whizzed past his head.

Albert dived for the pastor's scalp, but the pastor saw him coming. He ducked and Albert missed. Albert was furious, for he had waited so long for that one opportunity. With no chance of making a second swoop, he continued flying and did not stop until he landed in his man tree.

'Why am I so unlucky?' he cursed. 'Why, why, why?'

The police officer put the rifle back in the car, thinking he would return the next day to finish the job. 'That was one very lucky Magpie,' he mumbled.

However, Pastor Smith was determined to see that there would be no second chance. That afternoon, he returned to the park with a wildlife ranger. Together, they laid a bird trap, a spring-loaded net that could be launched into the air. Next, the ranger moved away with a trigger device in his hand, while the pastor stayed with the trap. The pastor was bait.

Albert watched the curious happenings from his throne but could see no danger in the net. Then, when the pastor squatted and removed his hat, Albert saw his chance. He launched himself, swooping carefully and with purpose. He had failed that morning because he had rushed. This time, he would land on the pastor's head. With beak and claw, he would inflict an injury.

Albert swooped, not bothered by the net that lay alongside the pastor. He wanted blood and success was almost his, but then the unexpected happened. The net flew into the air, and he crashed into it. Net and bird fell to the ground, and the ranger acted swiftly. Albert was extracted from the entanglement and thrown into a cage.

'You will look after him?' the pastor asked, feeling some guilt for having trapped a wild creature.

'Don't worry, he has a nice home waiting,' the ranger assured.

The drama was soon over, but there were witnesses. Muriel and Jenny watched from a nearby tree.

'Looks like you won't have to worry about the old bloke anymore,' Jenny laughed.

Muriel looked with disapproval at her sister. 'I will always worry because now I am worried about what will happen to him.'

The two Magpies perched in silence as the ranger's van drove off with Albert caged in the back.

41

JOURNEY'S END

Meanwhile, Max waited at the windmill, patiently hoping for rain. Each morning, he welcomed the dawn and listened for other Magpies doing the same. But there were no other Magpies. His carolling was the only carolling to be heard. Max thought that Alice might be about, and she would hear him and carol back, but there was only silence.

Time dragged slowly for each day seemed the same. Max amused himself by hunting for lizards and beetles, and by going for short flights to find other Magpies. But alas, he was all alone. The windmill was Max's only companion, and he sensed a strange bond growing between them, for they were both marooned on the edge of nowhere. All day, the windmill's blades would turn, and Max would hear him say, 'Please stay, please stay, please stay.' The same rhythmic groan was being repeated over and over again.

Max would look to the sky but see only blue, and he reasoned that the heat of the day was keeping the rain clouds away. He associated rain with the Dying Time, when the sky was grey, and the air was cold. Rain could be a fine drizzle, a sudden shower, or a daylong drenching. He had never known it to rain when the air felt warm. He guessed that Mother Nature had ruled it that way, and she would have to break her rule for rain to happen. Max needed a miracle.

***

The day was sunny, but the air felt strange. Then, in the late afternoon, a huge, black cloud drifted over the hills. It blocked out the sun, and then came flashes of lightning and deafening cracks of thunder. The wind howled, causing Max to hide under the water trough. Rain began to fall, and it was so heavy that the ground could not soak it in. Then, as suddenly as it all began, the rain stopped. The cloud moved on and the sun appeared once more. Max came out from hiding and felt the sun's warmth return. All about was cast in a soft, orange light, and there was an eerie silence broken only by the sound of dripping water. The air felt fresh.

Max had just witnessed the miracle he was hoping for, and he felt that Mother Nature was still with him on his journey. He watched the cloud as it drifted out over the plain, drenching the thirsty soil. Sometime later, a rainbow arched low across the flat terrain, but Max could still see the cloud in the distance. It glowed with flashes of lightning, and his keen ears could hear the faint rumble of far-off thunder.

Next morning, he bid the windmill farewell and set out once more. He was confident that he would find water on the plain, but he was wrong. The day was hot and only mud puddles remained. He soon became thirsty and the further he flew, the thirstier he became. He started to panic, but then hope appeared on the horizon. In the distance was another windmill, a kinsman to his friend. He flew towards it, but as he got closer, Crows came from nowhere. Some flanked him at the sides, while others flew behind and pecked at his feathers. The attack was a tactic that Magpies sometimes used against Crows, but these Crows were using it against him. He took shelter in a bush, but the Crows soon had his fragile fortress surrounded. Their leader stepped forward.

'Where do you think you are going?' cawed the leader.

Max thought quickly. 'Just dropping in for a friendly drink.' He hoped that his sociable intentions would see off the siege.

The leader laughed. 'Not at our windmill, now get going.'

I hate it when Crows laugh, thought Max, but he was outnumbered, and Homer had told him that the Crows never let other birds drink at their windmill. He had to appeal to their better nature.

'I will perish if I don't have water,' he pleaded.

Max's response brought a chorus of laughter from those that surrounded him, and then their leader gave a callous response.

'Don't worry, we will have a recycling crew standing by for when that happens.'

Max understood that joke this time. He should have known that Crows do not have a better side to their nature. Retreat was his only option. He left, and as he did, he felt the burn of their evil eyes watching him depart.

There was now no turning back, and he felt dizzy, no longer knowing which way he was going. He flew on, but he had to rest more often for his body ached. But each rest required another take-off, and they were becoming harder to perform. The heat from the ground was searing, and his thirst was unbearable. Then, when hope was almost gone, he saw what appeared to be a stand of tall trees in the distance. They were the only tall trees he had seen all day, and he thought that he might find water there, or at least, a perch high above the scorching ground. However, they could also be a mirage, for his mind was becoming muddled. He had to find out which, and he had just one last burst of flight left in him.

He flew towards the trees, thinking that they could vanish at any moment. As he drew closer, his confidence grew. The trees were real, but then he saw something strange. A bird flew from the trees. It flew high into the air, stalled, and then performed a steep dive.

What's Dopey doing all the way out here? thought Max, and then he answered his own question. *It's a mirage, a Dopey mirage.*

Max had become an expert at answering his own questions, which is a useful ability for a solo adventurer. It was an art he had perfected during his stay with the windmill.

He arrived at the trees and surveyed the scene. In their midst stood a house, and near the house stood a stable, and next to the stable stood a water trough, and next to the water trough stood a horse.

Max flew down and almost collapsed, his claws barely able to grip the rim of the trough. He bent over and took a beak full of water, worried that he might fall in.

'Be my guest,' said the horse.

'Sorry,' gasped Max, as he bent forward to take a second beak full.

'You must be a city boy,' the horse observed. He spoke in a slow drawl.

Max was sick of being called a city boy, but it took several gulps before his dry throat could manage a raspy reply.

'How can you tell?' he croaked.

'Country people ask.' The horse continued to speak slowly as he watched Max gulp the water. 'She's from the city you know.'

Max stopped. 'Who?'

They both looked up, which was difficult for Max, for he still felt dizzy. Max saw his Dopey mirage return. It flew high into the air, stalled, and then swooped towards them.

'Her up there, the one they call Dove Girl,' the horse drawled.

Max's muddled brain slowly processed the horse's words. *Did the horse just say, 'Dove Girl'?* Could it be that he had reached the end of his quest? Max did not feel excitement, he did not feel relief, he was feeling so ill.

The swooping bird landed next to the trough.

'Hi Horsey. Going to introduce me to your new friend?'

The horse put his head to the side and casually answered. 'Don't know much about him. He's a city boy, I think. Just flew in, looking for a drink.'

The two looked at Max, and then Alice's heart began to race. *Surely not. It couldn't be. Why doesn't he say something?* Alice could not believe what she was thinking. Her voice quivered as she uttered a single word.

'Maxie?'

'Hi Sis, long time no see. I think I need to find a branch to lie on.'

Alice turned to Horsey. 'Typical male. That is how he greets his long-lost sister.' Then she turned to Max. 'You never were the excitable type were you, Maxie?'

'Sorry, Sis, I am very excited, but I need to lie down. I think I am going to be sick.'

Alice hopped up onto the trough and took Max by the wing. 'Come on, Maxie. Birds don't lie on branches, but I know a nice cool place where you can rest.' She winked at Horsey. 'He always was a bit of a wimp.'

42

EDEN SPRINGS

Max had the longest sleep ever. He missed the Welcome of the Dawn and did not stir until a familiar peck jabbed him in the ribs. He woke, blinked his eyes, and shook his feathers.

'Still alive I see,' said Alice, having lost none of her charm when it came to waking her brother.

'Good morning, Sis, what's for breakfast?'

Alice smiled to herself. *Still the same old Maxie.* She felt the happiest that she could remember, and they dined that morning on an assortment of grasshoppers and beetles. Max scoffed them down.

'Don't eat too much,' Alice cautioned. 'You will be too full for treats.'

'What treats?' Max asked. He was puzzled, but Alice did not answer.

She put her claw on the beetle Max was about to eat. 'That's it. Stop eating,' she said. 'It's time for your grand tour.'

When did Alice get to be so bossy? Max wondered.

The lucky little beetle scurried away.

The house belonged to Adam and his wife, Evelyn, and they had a son, Colin. Horsey lived in the stable, and the farm drew its water from a natural spring. Adam and Evelyn called the place Eden Springs, which Horsey thought had something to do with a couple named Adam and Eve who lived long ago. In many ways, Eden Springs reminded Max of the wildlife park. There were Chooks and Ducks all over the place, running amok and getting into everything. They roosted in a large cage, which Evelyn closed at night to keep the occupants safe from marauding Foxes. Alice said that there had been discontent among the Ducks because Adam had promised them a pond, but they were still waiting.

She introduced Max to Bellow, the Cow. Bellow had a lean-to attached to Horsey's stable. Next, Max was shown Adam's vast vegetable garden. Adam was a vegetable grower, and Evelyn grew flowers and herbs. There was also a small flock of Sheep, and Evelyn used their wool to spin yarn. Alice said that she would introduce Max to the Sheep later.

'I doubt that I will remember all their names,' Max said.

Alice laughed. 'It won't be a problem, Maxie. They are mostly girls, but for some odd reason, they call each other Bruce.'

'What a strange coincidence,' Max commented. 'Do Emus live around here?'

'Some,' said Alice. 'Why do you ask?'

'Nothing important,' said Max. 'I was just thinking about a lost Emu I met on my travels. I think he may have come from these parts.'

Several Crows landed in the trees, and Max glared at them as he recalled his recent encounter at their windmill. Anger welled within him.

'I need to deal with those creeps,' he growled. 'There is no way that I am putting up with Crows around here.'

Alice could see that Max was still harbouring the impetuousness of his youth, and she did not want to see him start a fight that he could not win. She looked towards the house, for she could see movement. 'Come on, Maxie, forget the Crows. It's time for you to meet Colin.'

'I need to sort out the Crows,' Max growled.

'No, you are coming with me to meet Colin.'

'You certainly have got bossy,' Max mumbled, as he resolved to deal with the Crows later.

They flew to a veranda attached to the front of the house, where a young boy was sitting in a chair. He was thin and his skin was pale. The boy sat motionless, staring out at the trees, as if waiting for someone to appear.

Alice flew down and landed on the veranda floorboards while Max landed on the ground further away. His adventures had taught him to be cautious. The boy looked down at Alice, and his face beamed. Alice warbled a greeting, and the boy laughed.

'Come up here and meet Colin,' Alice called to Max.

'Are you sure it's safe?'

'Don't be a scaredy-cat,' quipped Alice.

Max hesitated, as he remembered Dopey's message. 'Oh, something else I must tell you. Don't let me forget.'

Max thought that a bad memory was something only visited on the old. His young memory was perfect, it was just that he sometimes had too many things to remember.

'I will remind you. Come on, Colin wants to meet you.'

Max flew onto the veranda, but he was not comfortable. He landed behind Alice, which meant that Colin would attack her first. He realised it was not what a bold adventurer would do, and he was debating the issue with his conscience when Alice raised the stakes. She perched on the armrest of Colin's chair. Max was being put to shame. It was then that he noticed that Colin's chair had large wheels attached. It was a wheelchair.

A Human appeared in the doorway behind the wheelchair. Max sounded the retreat but hesitated because the Human was looking back over his shoulder. The Human called to another who was inside the house.

'Evie, come and look at this. Colin has another Magpie. We don't see a Magpie in ten years, and then two turn up within months. It must be Climate Change.'

Evelyn came to the doorway just in time to see Max scurry for safety.

'Fly, Alice, there are Humans behind you,' he squawked.

Alice stayed put while Max took up a safe position further away.

Evelyn spoke. 'We do have two Magpies. Looks like I need to prepare some more treats, don't you think, Colin?'

Colin did not turn to talk to his mother. He sat rigid, looking at Alice, but Max could see his smile. Then he replied, 'Yeeees.'

Max's caution dimmed as he tried to fathom what it was he was seeing. Colin did not speak very well, and he was not moving that much either.

Alice looked at Max. 'Get up here, scaredy-cat, before I call you something worse.'

Max frowned. No girl was going to call him a scaredy-cat. He flew up and landed on the other arm of the wheelchair. Colin began to laugh, and his parents joined in. Max had never seen Humans laugh like that, but somehow, he had made all three of them laugh together. Charlie was right. Birds can make Humans happy, but he had no idea how the magic worked.

Evelyn brought out the most amazing food that Max had ever eaten, a mixture of bran and meat, with flavours he could never have imagined.

'Where do Humans find this great stuff?' Max asked.

Alice shrugged. 'Evelyn makes it; something she calls her special recipe.'

Max soon discovered that Colin did in fact have difficulty with both moving and talking. It was then that Alice told him her secret.

'Watch his eyes, and you will know what he is thinking. I know what he wants to say even though he cannot say it. I understand him better than his parents.'

Colin looked towards a white feather that was lying on the ground. He grunted, and Alice looked into his eyes. Alice then went over and held the feather in her beak. She flew into the air and released it, and Colin shook with laughter as the feather spun gently back to earth.

'I thought he wanted you to give him the feather,' Max said.

'No,' said Alice. 'He wanted me to make the feather fly. Fetch is a different game altogether.'

'You play games with him?'

'Yes, lots of them, and I am going to teach you how to play them as well.'

That evening, the siblings roosted in a tree that overhung Horsey's stable. They spoke quietly as they continued to exchange their many stories.

Alice told Max that Colin was always in his wheelchair, except for the times when he rode on Horsey's back. Adam would lead Horsey while Colin pointed to where he wanted to go. Colin loved his rides on Horsey.

'Isn't it strange,' said Alice. 'Horsey and I are the only ones who can make Colin laugh.'

'Charlie must have been right,' said Max.

'Who's Charlie?' queried Alice.

'You remember. My guru who lived in a box; the wise one you never went to see. He said that we make Humans happy.'

Alice thought for a moment and agreed. 'I think your guru is right,' she said. 'Humans seem to need us more than we need them.'

Suddenly, a cry came from within the house, and then a voice. 'Mummy's coming, Colin, Mummy's coming.'

Alice signalled Max not to speak. She listened until all was quiet again. 'Okay, Max, what were we just saying?' but Max had nothing to add on the matter.

Human behaviour was a mystery to him. He was still trying to work out if Humans were good or bad people. He changed the subject.

'Do you still want to find the Great River,' he asked.

Alice paused before answering, listening to make sure that Colin was no longer in distress.

'No, my special place is here,' she said.

Max looked puzzled. 'What makes this place special?'

Alice looked towards the house. 'This is where I am needed. This is where I am special.'

The conversation fell silent. Max was puzzled by his sister's change in ambition. He thought about everything that had happened that day, and about Alice's delight when told that Dopey had returned from the dead. 'Only Dopey could pull that one off,' she had said.

Max's mind began to drift, and then he remembered Dopey's message.

'Dopey said to tell you that you are not a scaredy-cat.'

'Oh, is that what that was about,' said Alice. 'Silly Dopey, I know I am not a scaredy-cat, but I will never be as crazy as he is.'

'No,' said Max. 'Only Dopey could get himself abducted by aliens.'

'What?' squawked Alice. Her reaction rang out from the tree, causing a voice to come from below.

'Would you guys be quiet up there. There is a horse down here trying to get some sleep.'

'Sorry Horsey,' said Max, giving Alice a light jab in the ribs.

'Actually, his name is Gerald,' Alice giggled.

'Then I will apologise to him in the morning,' whispered Max.

'It's okay, he prefers to be called Horsey.'

'Go to sleep, Alice.'

'Did Dopey really get abducted by aliens?'

Max did not reply. Alice gave another giggle and then there was silence.

Down below, Horsey sighed, 'Peace at last.'